THEN THERE WAS RED

a fairytale mystery

Book Cover designed by Ellen ES Ceely operating with Unfinished Publishing

Book Art by Corrie Bergmann, https://corriebergmann.com/

First edition 2025

eBook ISBN 978-1-962016-10-0
Color Paperback ISBN 978-1-962016-09-4
B&W Paperback ISBN 978-1-962016-12-4

10 9 8 7 6 5 4 3 2 1

For everyone, like Wolf,
who has been judged by how they look
or for who their parents were.

For those, like Red,
who are afraid to speak up.

For those, like Drina,
who never give up hope.

Your stories matter.
You matter.

WOLF'S SHACK

FELL VILLAGE

FLETCHER'S

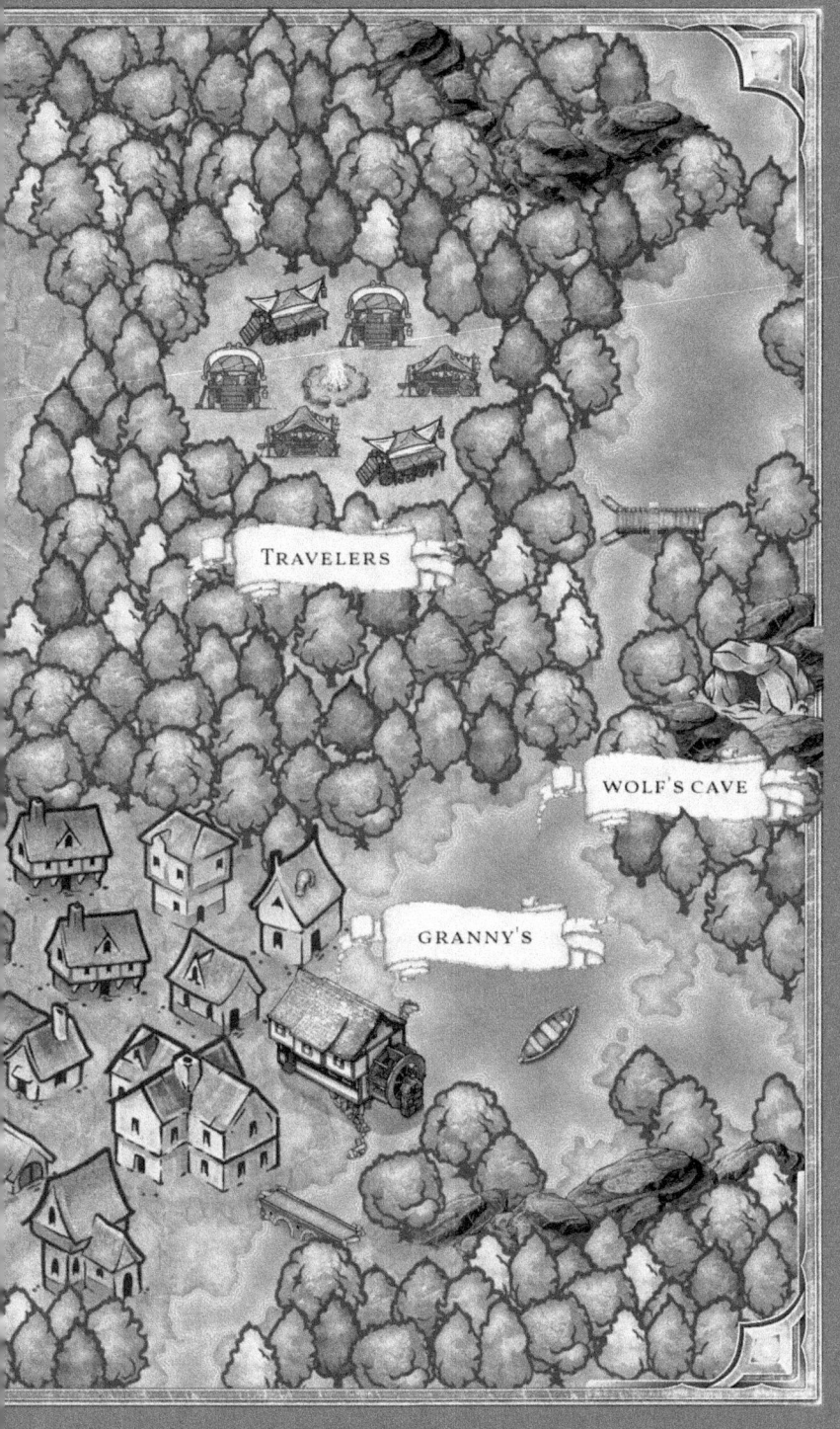

70 years Earlier
Celeste, 13

Autumn

The camp is quiet. Papa made me this journal. No one else will be friends with me, so I'll write my secrets down here. You can be my friend, my confidante, and my sister. I want out. I want more than this stupid, stinking camp. I don't want to live in a wagon.

A traveling book master recently sold me a book about a princess who lived in a castle. She had a giant bed with long, red curtains. I want that. I want to be the princess. I want servants to bring me my meals and clean my room and do laundry.
No one can know. They'll all laugh at me and tell me I'm being foolish if I tell them about my dream.

Frederick has been working on something. He spends hours on it. Every time I try to look, he hides it away. He's so handsome. His short, curly hair falls over his forehead just so. He's tall and strong and such a powerful wolf for his age.

I told him we should get married when we grow up. All he did was turn away and shake his head. I'm not giving up though. He needs to see me as a woman instead of a girl. I can make it happen. I can make him fall in love with me.

Then the two of us can escape this life and become important.

1

ONCE UPON A TIME, there lived a murderer. Once upon a time, Granny was murdered. And everyone believed I did it. The only problem is, I wasn't there. I was lying unconscious in the woods with no one to vouch for me.

Throbbing in the back of my head woke me. I tried opening my eyes but quickly closed them again.

Lying face down on the forest floor, I pushed myself over onto my back, eyes still tightly shut against the rays of sun sifting through the trees. Gritting my teeth against the pain exploding in my head, I took a deep breath and let it out slowly. *One. Two. Three.* I counted, waiting for my pulse to slow.

The chirping of birds from above, the scent of decaying leaves and moss underneath - the sounds and smells of home. A slight breeze ran over my skin and the hairs on my arms prickled. Autumn had arrived early this year.

Trying to distract myself with what I could feel around me, I waited for the pain to subside. The damp, cool air revived me, softening the nausea I was trying to ignore.

What in the moon's name happened last night? I wondered, spreading my arms out to either side as I tried to recall the events of the night before. I'd been walking home from checking my traps. I'd made it over the foot bridge and through town without anyone even noticing me. *Always a welcome event.* I thought, the bitter relief taking over.

But what happened once I left the road for the cover of the forest? I was almost home. The moon was high and full. All I wanted was to be home, to tumble into bed. My thoughts raced as I took in a quick breath. *A twig snapped, then everything went black.* The pain in my head soared with my adrenaline, panic overwhelming me.

Did someone follow me? I wondered. It wouldn't have been the first time. I'd known more than my fair share of bullies in my lifetime. My thoughts drifted back to the first sneer I'd ever seen on the face of a villager, the first time a complete stranger spat in my direction.

"Cursed dogs!" the toothless old man had said, shaking his cane at me as I clutched my mother's hand, and she dragged me through the village square. "It would be better to see you burn, boy!" His eyes shone with the fire I knew he wished he could throw me into.

My mother's clenched jaw and silent tears had been etched into my memory.

Four years old. I thought. *I was only four years old. I hadn't even turned yet. I didn't even understand what it meant to turn.* Flipping to my side, I pushed the memory away and tried to open my eyes again.

The sunlight hurt my eyes, but not like before. I grimaced and blinked. *I need water. A little food. If I can make it to my hut, then I can go to the village and talk to the sheriff.* Reporting what had happened to me wouldn't do any good.

But why knock me unconscious and leave me? I wondered, realizing with relief that nothing had been taken off me and I didn't feel as though I'd been beaten in my unconscious state. *Was their spite so great they only wished to incapacitate me, but felt I wasn't worth the effort of beating or robbing?* I almost laughed at the idea. *Maybe it was a stranger.* The hope was silly.

Slowly, I rolled onto my stomach with my hands beneath me and raised myself to my hands and knees. Gritting my teeth I clenched my eyes shut against the new pain searing through my neck. Soon it relented and I pushed myself up onto my knees, opening my eyes again and looking around.

The forest swam at the edges of my vision, but another deep breath steadied me and I found a nearby tree to reach out and touch.

The rough bark of the ancient oak was comforting against my right palm, steady and grounding. Pushing against the tree, I stood up, leaning against it to keep from falling. I wrapped my right arm around it as I closed my eyes again and felt the back of my head with my left hand.

A large knot responded angrily as my hand came in contact with it.

"Curse!" I hissed, immediately removing my hand to let it hang by my side. The throbbing slowed and I opened my eyes again. Looking around, I spotted my things on the ground - an empty trap and a sack full of meat I'd need to discard.

Not only was I left unconscious, and they didn't think me worth robbing, now I'll also go hungry. Gritting my teeth, I took a step forward to gather my things. The pain was almost insufferable, but the more steps I took, grasping trees as I moved through the forest, the more stable my feet began to feel.

I reached the clearing where my cabin sat, decrepit and small. Watching it from within the safety of the trees, I waited, paranoia taking over my senses.

Nothing moved, no noises came from within. All I saw was the cracked window and the peeling yellow paint on the door. *Yellow: the color of cowardice, the color of my eyes under a full moon.* I thought, the old man spitting at me as a child coming back to mind again. *Full moons like the one last night.*

The door had been yellow ever since I could remember. A physical symbol of shame to anyone who ventured near.

After a few more minutes, I pushed away from the tree line and made my way inside the cabin, poking my head inside the door before I pushed it open.

Everything looked as I'd left it the afternoon before. Every rusted pot and pan hung on a hook, the remnants of my stale bread sat on the table, and the hearth sat cold and empty of flame.

Breathing a sigh of relief, I pushed the door open and slumped against the door frame. *Water.* I thought, dropping the sack of spoiled meat and the empty trap on my doorstep. *Then a little stale bread.*

I made my way over to the table, practically falling into my decrepit old chair. Scooping some water out of the bucket beside the hearth, I took a long drink.

My throat cooled as the water slid down my throat. Nausea stilled and turned to nauseating hunger. I drank my fill and reached for the stale bread, breaking off a hunk of it to stuff in my mouth.

All my trapping is gone. Pelts, meat - what did they want from me? I mulled over my aching head. *Was it just spite?* Bitterness welled up inside as I considered the reasoning. My bread disappeared sooner than I'd hoped. Sighing, I looked around the cabin.

The broken cot I slept on, a stool with my extra clothes on it, the broom I never used, and my bow and arrows all stared back at me. Outside, the birds chirped and the trees rustled.

"What do I do now?" I asked the room. My stomach answered me with a growl. "Go check my traps again and hope luck is in my favor. Got it." I said, staring down at the offending noisemaker.

Lifting a tentative hand back to my head, I winced as it made contact with the bump.

Feeling around for blood, I realized the object hadn't broken the skin. *Small mercies.*

"Well, if I'm to go back through the village to check my traps again, then I should probably change first," I announced to the stool holding my clothes.

When did I start talking to inanimate objects? I wondered. *Five years is a long time to live alone, but at this rate, I'll be as crazy as the day is long by the time I reach maturity.* My heart ached at the thought of five years. Five years since my mother had left me, too weak to fight the illness.

No one had cared. Most inhabitants of the village hadn't even noticed until weeks passed, and my mother was no longer around. No one said anything to me. The village left me to live however I wanted at twelve years old. *They probably hoped I'd die.*

Pushing myself up, I leaned on the table for a second to catch my balance. The water and bread had eased the dizziness and upset stomach I was experiencing. Shuffling over to the stool, I quickly pulled off my mud-covered clothes and pulled on the less disgusting shirt and pants waiting for me.

I moved slowly throughout the cabin, taking a couple more ladlesful of water as I prepared to leave. Grabbing an empty sack, I shoved my cloak inside it and slung it over my left shoulder. Next, I grabbed my trap, my bow and arrows, a floppy hat, and the sack of rotten meat. Closing the door behind me, I walked through the forest back toward the village.

I dropped the rotten meat in a ditch along the way, far enough away from my cabin to not attract unwanted visitors. The sun was rising overhead, bringing on the noonday heat. Even beneath the shade of the trees, I could feel the sun, and I was thankful I'd remembered to grab my hat.

I reached the main road before another hour had passed. Making my way into the village, I adjusted my bow strap as houses came into view. An eerie silence hung in the air. Nothing moved, no one spoke. I looked around expectantly, waiting to see someone.

The streets were empty.

Odd. I thought, frowning. *At midday the streets should be bustling with gossip and work. Where did everyone go?* I stopped to look around again. Tilting my head to one side, I called on one of the few good things my curse had given me: a keen sense of hearing.

I shut my eyes and focused. The subtle murmur of too many voices all speaking at once drifted toward me. *It's coming from the mill.* The hairs on the back of my neck began to prickle a warning. *Nothing good comes from the mill. Stay away from there. Go the long way around.*

I stood rooted to the ground for a moment, wondering if I should investigate or listen to my gut. *That's the way I need to go anyway. What's the big deal? No one will be paying any attention to me. They're all focused on whatever's happening there.*

Adjusting my bow strap again, more from nerves than necessity, I forced my legs to turn toward the mill and follow the murmur of the crowd. The closer I got, the louder the murmuring became. As I rounded the last bend, what appeared to be every last villager came into view, huddled closely by the front mill door.

Pushing myself up onto my toes, I tried to see what was going on, but the crowd was too dense. Just as I was about to turn away and continue with my own business, a woman turned around.

Smiling, I opened my mouth to ask her what was happening, but the words froze in my throat as her eyes grew large and she shrank away from me.

"You!" the woman screamed, pointing at me with one hand as she pushed against the people next to her. "You did it!" she screamed even louder, the crowd around her hushing and turning to look.

I took a tentative step forward, one hand held out as the questions died on my tongue. Dozens of eyes met my gaze with hatred and fear.

"Murderer!" cried someone from the middle of the crowd. I shook my head and stumbled backward. *They must be mistaken.*

"Monster!" screamed another.

You need to run. My brain told my legs, but my legs seemed unable to understand the command.

"Cut off his head and burn his bones!" called the woman, still pointing at me. "He came to exact his revenge in the dark of the night and dares return, pretending to be innocent!"

For a split second, no one moved or spoke. They stared at me and I stared back. Then the crowd surged forward as one.

Unsure of what else to do, and certain my death was imminent if I didn't, I ran as fast as possible.

Autumn

Frederick keeps working on his secret project. I managed a quick peek before he caught me and went to hide it. It's some sort of box he's carving with a whole bunch of little pieces. I pretended I hadn't seen what he was making when he spotted me. If he's just making a box, then I don't see what the big deal is.

Papa told me I need to stop daydreaming and grow up. He says it's time for me to understand that this is what life is. I didn't argue. I nodded and took the laundry to the river to wash.

Mama sat there the whole time; her eyes still distant, like she's lost in some other world. She's been this way ever since last winter, when Theo died. It was an accident. I didn't know the ice would break beneath his weight. She stares at me and through me.

My deepest desire is to run away. I wish I could leave the laundry by the river and flee today. But I don't have any money yet. I need some coins to take with me if I want to survive. Dying is not the way I want to escape.

I caught another glimpse of Frederick's box. It has a wolf howling at the moon carved into it. He's been fiddling with all the little pieces lately, pushing here and there to see what happens. I'm not sure I understand what he's making.

Last night, under the full moon, I peered out of our wagon.

Frederick couldn't see me. It was too dark and he was busy. He sat with the box in his hands, staring at it while he angled it toward the bright moonlight. His lips kept moving, but I couldn't hear what he said.

What is he doing? What is he trying to make? I must find out. Maybe it will be the key to my freedom. Maybe he and I can leave sooner than I expect.

2

I DARED NOT LOOK back. The roar of the crowd followed close behind me. Slipping in and out of alleyways, I called on the blood of wolves deep within me, that same blood I'd spent my entire life denying, begging for speed.

"Murderer!"

"Catch him!"

"Stop that vile dog!"

What on earth happened? My thoughts raced as I ducked down another alleyway, having made up my mind to head toward the footbridge and cross the river. My head pounded, dull pain reminding me of the night before.

Someone set me up. The realization hit me, and I gritted my teeth in anger, pushing forward with a little more speed. The voices were growing dimmer, their cries fainter and more desperate.

The only sound still following me was the shallow breathing and light footsteps of one pursuer.

As I set foot on the bridge, I felt a hand scrape the back of my shirt, wrenching at the fabric but failing to grab hold of it. Without a second thought, I whirled on my assailant with all the force I had, hitting him square in the jaw as he tried to stop himself but failed.

As he fell to the side, nearly hitting his head on the footbridge railing, I recognized the Sheriff. He groaned into the dirt and rocks. Not daring to wait for him to get up, I turned and fled across the bridge. The trees on the other side soon enveloped me, and I ducked into their comforting cover.

I climbed over the boulders just as I had dozens of times as a child, running from bullies. I knew every crook and crevice to use to swing myself deftly up and over. Plunging through the river's little side pool, the water washed over me with relief. My breath was ragged and my steps unsteady by the time I reached the opposite shore.

For a brief second, I gazed up at the steep rockface before me, my heart racing while my muscles burned. It had been a while since I'd visited the cave. *Here's hoping it's still empty and no one uses it for anything.* I thought, jumping to grab the crevices in the rock as my feet found their place. I shimmied upwards, remembering every foothold and crevice like I'd climbed it yesterday.

Finally, I reached the top and pulled myself over the edge. The narrow entrance to the cave loomed before me, a comforting reminder of all the times I'd hidden there as a child. Staying low to the rockface, I slipped inside the cave and sank to the ground.

Who died? I wondered. Remembering which house the crowds had been gathered around, my heart skipped a beat as terror flooded me. *The mill. Granny's house. Someone murdered Granny - or Red?* Shutting my eyes, I listened intently for anyone who might've followed me as I continued to try to catch my breath.

Now I'm soaked from head to foot. I have no food, no blankets, and I dare not return home. The relief of the cool water had turned to dread as the cold rock at my back bit through my tunic and cloak.

"You have time," I told myself, my voice barely above a whisper. "Remove your clothes and dry them on the rocks before the sun goes down."

Before my limbs stiffened with cold, I undid the sack and drew out my cloak. Crawling back out onto the rockface and into the sunshine, I wrung out the cloak as best I could and laid it over the hot rock.

As the wind brushed over my wet clothing, I looked around for and found a few loose stones to place on the corners of the cloak so it wouldn't fly away in the breeze.

My shirt followed, but my pants remained in place as I chose to hunker down atop the hot stone and allow them to dry on me rather than end up naked as well as vulnerable.

Closing my eyes, I tried to ignore the growing growl of my stomach. The throbbing in my head had eased again, but not disappeared.

"What am I going to do?" I asked the wind as the trees swayed beside me. "They'll never believe me. Why would they? I'm the grandson of the most notorious murderer their village has ever known."

And their hero was just murdered. My mind whispered to me. I groaned, rubbing my face with my hands in frustration. *The woman who executed your grandfather and made the murders stop has now been murdered herself.*

Thinking back to the night before, I tried and failed to remember anything about who might have attacked me. *Why bother?* I realized, pushing myself up onto my elbows and blinking at the sunlight.

Why not just commit the murder and blame me? I puzzled over the question, trying to understand. *The entire village would believe it was me at the drop of a pin. Why go to all that extra trouble? I have no alibi.*

I looked out over the treetops, watching them sway in the sunshine. No answers came to mind. Shades of red, orange, and yellow fluttered back at me, the forest still silent. I sighed. My muscles relaxed, and I realized how sore my entire body was.

"What am I going to do?" I asked again. Realizing the front of my pants was dry, I turned over onto my stomach, resting my chin on my hands. "I could run," I whispered into the trees. "Find some other village where no one knows me. Sleep in the woods. Start over." It wasn't the first time I'd considered leaving my home.

As long as I was the grandson of my grandfather, Fell Village would never accept me as their own. *Why did I stay so long to begin with?* I knew the answer before I'd even finished asking the question. *Because it's the only home I've ever known. It's the only piece of mother I have left.* I swallowed the lump forming in my throat and shook my head.

"I could surrender." I guffawed at the words leaving my mouth. *I'd be dead before I even told them I was surrendering.* There was no point. Giving myself up would be no worse than being caught. *They would never believe me. In their minds, I'm already guilty. There would be no trial.*

"Well then," I told myself, shifting onto my elbows and pursing my lips. "The only other option I have is to stay in hiding and figure out what happened."

The truth. Just say it: the truth. But the words wouldn't form in my mouth. *I may have no memory of who hit me, but I also have no memory of last night.* The hurtful part of me spoke up, the part of me that doubted my ability to fight off the moon and the blood coursing through my veins. *What if I did it?*

I considered the idea for a second, a sick feeling in my stomach. "If you'd done it, you'd have been covered in more than the dirt and mud of the forest." I scolded myself and sat up. "Get a grip."

Reaching over, I felt my shirt and realized it was dry. Pulling it over my head, I turned the cloak over and placed it on a new, warm spot. *There's only an hour of daylight left.* I secured the cloak with rocks again.

Once the sun sets and the moon emerges, they'll abandon their search. There was no guarantee that this would happen, but I wanted to hope. *I can go hunting then. I can check my traps. Maybe even find a way back to my home and get a few things.*

I shook my head. *That's foolish. They might pause the manhunt for the night, but they'll stake out your home.* I sighed again, exhaustion washing over me. *Food. That must be your focus. Food to eat.* I nodded in agreement with myself, staring out at the trees and waiting for the sun to go down.

No more decisions would be made until I'd eaten some food.

I woke to the sound of voices, shivering and stiff on the top of the rocks. Stifling a groan, I pushed myself up onto my hands and knees, trying to shake away the sleep in my eyes. *When did I drift off?* I wondered, feeling around for my cloak.

"Oy, you don't think he went and climbed up these rocks then, do you?" The man's voice was close and the moon was bright. Instead of pulling my cloak, I slowly lowered down onto my stomach.

"Climb rocks? Who ever heard of a stinking dog climbing rocks!" Another man responded. "What's a dog going to do on top of a rock?

Jump into the trees and start jumping from branch to branch like a squirrel?"

"Well he wasn't in his cursed dog form now was he?"

"You think too much."

The conversation devolved into bickering as I tried to decide what to do. *If I stay here, they might climb up and find me. But if I move, they might see me in the moonlight and find me.* My skin tingled with anticipation in the moonlight.

You could change. The idea came to me with a mixture of excitement and dread. I'd only ever changed twice in my life.

The first time was when I came of age, before I knew what was happening to me. The second time was when my mother died. *Not even when the boys were chasing me with knives in their hands did I change.* I argued with the voice telling me to do it.

"Well, I don't much care what you think," the first man's voice grew loud and angry. He was sputtering. "I want to catch the cursed dog and kill him before he can hurt anyone else. If you don't care about keeping our village safe from monsters like him, then you can wait here!"

Scraping against the base of the rock met my ears. *It's now or never.* The voice said. *Run, change, or keep lying there like an idiot and get caught.*

Closing my eyes, I leaned into the tingling across my skin. My body warmed as I sank into the pool of waning moonlight above. My bones shifted as I transformed. I was in pain, but it was glorious.

Every scent increased in intensity; every sound became louder. I opened my eyes to a world so vivid and clear my breath caught in my throat. The world stretched out for miles in every direction, visible to me in the dead of night.

As the sound of the climbing man grew closer, the pain in my body disappeared. Crawling out of my clothing, I scooped it up into my mouth and dragged it toward the cave. Returning on quiet paws I did the same with my cloak, sinking deep into the crevice to wait beside my things. I had a narrow but clear view of the rock outside.

My stomach roared with hunger as a shadowy figure pull itself over the top of the rocks, panting for breath.

"Come on, then Matthew," the man growled to his companion. "Hand up a torch so I can have a look around." A light flickered and I winced against its harshness. His face came into view. From the mustache on his lip to the hat on his head, I recognized him as the blacksmith.

Sinking to the ground, I watched him, ready to pounce if required. *It would only prove their belief that I'm guilty.* I told myself. *Does it matter?* The other part of me argued back. *If he attacks and you don't defend yourself, it won't matter what the truth is. You'll be dead.*

He stalked around the rockface, somehow missing the cave entrance entirely or believing it was a mere crevice.

"Well, Andrew?" A voice called from below. "Do you see anything?"

"No," the Blacksmith growled back. "Must've heard us talking and left before I got up here. Smells like wet dog. I'm coming back down."

The hair along my neck bristled as he turned his back to me. *You could attack him now, take him out, push him off balance. He'll topple to his death. They'd never know it was you.*

Shutting my eyes, my mother's face came into view as she cleaned my split lip and scraped knuckles. I swore that I would get even with the village boys if it was the last thing I managed to do.

"The only thing keeping you from becoming who they believe you are is you refusing to be anything other than the real you." She'd paused, tilting my angry eyes up to meet hers.

"Don't allow them to make you into the monster they believe you to be. Continue to show up as the boy I know you are: compassionate, kind, intelligent, and brave. Do not become their monster. Don't give them the satisfaction."

Tears stung at the edge of my wolf eyes. It took every bit of strength I had left inside of me to ignore the voice urging me to attack and wait, unmoving, as the man launched himself back down the rocks and out of sight.

I am not the monster they believe me to be.

70 years Earlier
Celeste, 13

<u>Winter</u>

Frederick talked to me today. He didn't just tolerate my presence, but talked to me. In complete sentences. I'm making progress. He told me he hopes to be an inventor who combines magic with his skill in carving. I told him I think he's the most handsome and talented child of the moon in the camp. He blushed when I said that and shook his head. But I made him smile.

My plan is working. He'll fall in love with me, and we can run away together.

Book! Frederick showed me his box. I could hardly contain my excitement. It's been weeks of flattery and talking and listening, but he finally showed me his box. He says it's almost finished, then he swore me to secrecy.

He believes he can make the box a tool of magic. He's decided under the next full moon that he'll spill a drop of his blood in the carving and transfer the power of his shifting to the box.

I can't say I understand the point. Not wanting to offend him, of course, I didn't ask. I'm not a shifter.

Maybe there's a reason you'd want to hand over control? I would die to have that kind of control over someone else.

Frederick swore me to secrecy. No one wants to hear me talk anyway. He's my only friend, and I made sure to tell him that. He said I can come watch him the night of the full moon. I plan to.

The spell worked. I've never wanted something so badly in my whole life.

Frederick used his blood on the box to transfer his ability to transform. He had me help. I thought the spell would be fancier, but it turns out he'd already done the bulk of the magic. All I had to do was hold the box with a drop of his blood in the carving, then look to the moon and command him to transform.

Is magic really this simple? As soon as I spoke the words, he transformed. He turned into a wolf right before my eyes. I felt...powerful. So powerful! To hold the power of the man I love in my hands? It was incomparable to anything I've ever experienced.

I confess I wanted to keep the box. But, of course, I couldn't. After I commanded him to transform back to his human form, he dressed and took it from me. He looked both disturbed and excited about what had happened.

Maybe I can convince him to run away with me now.

3

M Y BODY ACHED WITH hunger. Right before sunrise, voices disappeared, and I
crawled out from the safety of my cave, still in
wolf form. I managed to catch the most anemic
rabbit I'd ever seen. Unable to start a fire and
afraid to change into my human form, I ate it
raw.

Maybe I am the beast they believe me to be.
The disgusted part of my brain told me as I
tore into the warm rabbit, too hungry to wait
until I got back to the cave. *None of them would
eat a raw animal. None of them would turn
into a deadly wolf.* My stomach growled, and
I pushed away the thoughts as I took another
bite.

My meal was done far too soon, and long before my stomach was full. But it was enough to
sustain me. Digging a hole, I buried the carcass

and covered it back up, aware that the blood and bits of fur would still be noticeable.

Creeping to the edge of the water, I drank my fill and let the water wash away the blood on my mouth.

The forest was silent. The search party must have retired until dawn, recognizing it was too dark and they were too tired to properly search for me. *Small mercies.*

The reflection of the moon caught my eye in the water. I studied it before looking up to view the real thing. *The moon sees me. The moon believes who I am. It doesn't fear me. It's not ashamed of me.* The thoughts came in rapid fire. I was exhausted, but the cool light kissed my fur and calmed something deep inside me.

The most animalistic urge I'd ever felt welled up from deep within. *What would it be like to howl at the moon? What would it be like to sing back to the one who gives me my strength? The creator of my greatest strength and worst weakness?*

Fighting the urge to make noise as alarm bells went off in my head, I looked back down at the water, ready to take another drink. The face of a wolf stared back at me, deep green eyes and black fur reflecting in the water.

Killer. Monster. Beast. The insults ran through my head. *Never a name, just a face of someone - or something - they hate.* A slow blink of my eyes brought me out of my reverie. *Pity will get you nowhere.* It was time to move back to somewhere safe.

Slinking through the woods, I climbed back to my cave and curled up on top of my cloak. Exhaustion won out as sunlight broke through the trees. Unable to fight it anymore, I fell asleep.

The next day passed in a blur. Search parties crawled all over the woods. My body ached from crouching in the dark cave, ready to pounce if someone entered and found me. The men's voices drifted up over the rocks and into the cave.

"They found bits of fur and traces of blood in the forest."

"Bastard caught a rabbit, did he?"

"Barbaric, if you ask me. Pure dog. That's all he is. A beast."

My stomach growled at the memory of the rabbit. *So small. Not enough to fill me then. Still hungry.* Broken thoughts drifted through my mind as my mouth watered at the thought of food.

"The coward must be hiding somewhere."

"Or he's run off somewhere to terrorize another village."

"Maybe he fell in the water and drowned?"

"We can only hope. He can only hope too. Would be a better death than what I've got planned for him."

Crude laughter followed as the voices drifted out of hearing. A growl started in my throat before I could stop it. *Never been a wolf this long.* I swallowed, shifting on my sore limbs as I worked to contain the instinctual noise.

The sun will be down soon. You can go hunting again. The thought made me antsy. *Maybe I can catch more this time. Something bigger. Something with plenty of meat to enjoy before daylight.*

Visions of rabbits ran through my imagination. I caught them, ripped them apart with my teeth, and devoured their flesh. The drool was uncontrollable now. *I'll catch more than one and eat my fill. Maybe I'll even catch a hunter before he can catch me.*

New visions clouded my thoughts, and I shrank internally as I realized what I was considering. *A desire for the flesh of man has never been mine.* I scolded myself as I stared out the small cave opening at the setting sun. *That's not me. I am not the beast they want me to be.*

The visions, however, didn't listen. As voices drifted out of earshot and the sun gave way to darkness, my mind devoured more than one hunter. With each mental kill, my blood ran hot. The moon rose outside, beckoning me to exit my self-chosen cage.

Maybe I should turn back. Some small part of myself broke through, a part I recognized as fully me. But in a flash, it had been hushed and buried. All the voices had disappeared, so I exited the cave and went in search of another rabbit.

Only a rabbit. I told myself. *Only another animal.* But my mind struggled to distinguish the difference between the rabbit and the hunter as I became, once more, the hunter myself.

Pain throbbed in my temples as I tried to open my eyes. I gritted my teeth and squinted as panic consumed me. Soft blankets surrounded me. Underneath, on top. Through crinkled eyes, a red blur came into view. *Red. Red is the enemy, the hunter, the pursuer.*

My panic grew, and I struggled to sit up, gasping as the pain in my head grew worse. I collapsed back into the softness beneath me, still gritting my teeth to keep from screaming.

"Hush now, child." A rich voice met my ears. A woman's voice, deep and soothing. *What must she sound like when she sings?* The thought came out of nowhere.

"I can sing for you if it will soothe your pain." Her voice held a smile.

I froze, my heart racing and my breath growing shallow. I tried to open my eyes again, but to no avail. A cool cloth was laid over my forehead, and a soft hand brushed back my hair.

"You're safe, boy. Go back to sleep. No one will harm you here." Her hand continued to stroke my head as the coolness of the cloth made me unclench my teeth.

"Under the moon and stars we sing, Within the dark of night we bring, What little cheer we have to give, With every breath we have to live."

Sobs threatened in my throat as my fear began to disappear. *The moon.* I thought, remembering the vividness of it as I'd watched it in my wolf form. *My wolf form.* I thought, registering I was no longer the animal but the human. *How? When did that happen?* I wanted answers, but the soothing cloth reminded me of my exhaustion, and I felt myself drifting off.

"Answers will find you, boy. Go to sleep. You'll find me right beside you when you wake."

With a new cool cloth on my eyes and forehead, and one more brush of her hand through my hair, I was asleep.

When I woke again, the cloth was gone, and so was the pain. I turned onto my back and opened my eyes slowly. *No pain.* I blinked, grateful to have relief.

Above me hung a rainbow of cloth strung over poles. Red, teal, yellow - every color imaginable had been strung together to decorate whatever odd structure I was lying in.

"Good morning, child." The rich voice interrupted my awe. I started and turned to my left.

A face full of wrinkles met my gaze. Her crooked teeth broke through her beaming smile. Piercing black eyes sparkling with a joy I'd never seen before gazed into my own eyes as though they were peering into my soul. Wavy hair as dark as night drifted down the woman's back, braids and feathers and dried flowers adorning her like a crown.

I blinked again, wondering if I was still dreaming. "Who are you?" I asked, my dry throat sending me into a coughing fit.

The woman's warm hand lifted my head and held water to my lips. "Drink." She commanded. I obeyed without hesitation. *If they wanted me dead, they would've already killed me.* My coughing soon subsided, and the woman laid my head back on the softness beneath me.

"My name is Drina, defender of mankind." Her sideways smile and the wink she gave me caught me off guard. "What is your name, child?" She prodded, still staring at me with those piercing eyes.

I looked away, unable to meet her gaze. "I have no name," I spoke softly, testing out my voice again. I studied the embroidery on her red dress. *Red. That's what I saw the first time I awoke here.*

"You have a name," she replied after a moment. "You simply do not wish to embrace it as your own."

My eyes shot up to meet hers as indignation burned in my chest. I opened my mouth to speak, but words left me at the look of pure compassion on her face.

"Wolf," I muttered, dropping my eyes again.

"Wolf may be a little on the snout," she replied with a small laugh. "However, it is nothing to be ashamed of, dear soul."

I couldn't look at her. I didn't want to look at her. "How did I get here?" I asked, my eyes landing on an embroidered pattern of stars on her dress sleeve. "Where am I?"

"It took a bit of convincing, a lot of chasing, and some coaxing with a large amount of food," she said. "But you finally came around, ate your fill, and fell asleep in the cage we created to catch you."

My eyes shot up to meet hers, wide with fear. I tried pushing myself up into a sitting position. *Maybe I can overpower her. It's not too late to leave.* But my arms felt like jelly and my whole body ached.

"Hush, child." She said, pushing me back down with very little force. "No one here wants to harm you. We caught you for your own good." She smoothed back the hair that had fallen over my brow.

My heart pounding, I stared at her, waiting for better answers.

"The villagers were closing in. You were bound to be captured if we didn't intervene. That or commit murder out of desperation and starvation." Her sharp eyes held mine, her look both full of pity as well as rebuke. "We gave you food and gave you a safe place to hide. The villagers searched our camp before they searched anywhere else. They'll not be looking for you here. Do you understand?"

Blinking at her, I tried to take in everything she'd told me. "I'm in a camp? A camp of who? Who are you?"

Drina sighed. "Did your mother - moon and stars rest her soul - ever tell you about the wagon people?" she asked, offering me another sip of water. I nodded my head in response to her question while raising it to take the offered water. "What did she say?"

"She told me stories of an ancient people, people who wandered these lands before the villages were settled," I said, frowning as I re-membered the stories my mother had told me on cold nights when the wind wouldn't stop and the fire in our hearth couldn't compete with the gusts slipping through the cracks in our walls.

"Aye, my boy." She gestured to our surroundings. "That's us. Welcome to our clan of wagon people." She tilted her head upwards and laughed, hands still raised. A cold sweat broke out on my forehead, and I closed my eyes again, wondering if I'd truly woken up or if I was trapped in a wagon with someone insane.

"I've not lost my mind, child," Drina said, abruptly interrupting my thoughts. "Not any more than you have lost yours for choosing to become the beast who resides within you." Her hands lowered, and she tilted her head to one side. "Tell me, how do you feel now that you're human again?"

"My whole body hurts," I said without hesitation.

"My question had nothing to do with whether or not your body hurts," she replied, shaking her head. "I asked you how you feel. In here." She laid one hand on her heart while pointing to her head with the other.

Tears threatened to fall as I realized the truth. "I feel as though I've lost someone I love and can't find them," I said, gritting my teeth to keep back the tears.

"Aye," she said, her eyes filling with tears. "So it is with all travelers who must abandon their other half." She laid one hand on my chest. "So it is with you, child of the moon," she laid her other hand on her chest. "As it is with me, child of the stars."

"What are you saying?" I asked, my heart pounding in my ears.

"Your mother was a traveler. So are you. You are not only among friends, my boy. You are home. With family."

Winter
I HATE FREDERICK.

I told him I loved him. I begged him to run away with me. He laughed in my face and told me I was a child, nothing more than his annoying little friend.

There's no use in caring about having coins anymore. I plan to leave as soon as I can. I'll wait until the moon is at its darkest. Then I'll steal the box and leave. I'll run to the north. I've never been that way. I can follow the road to a town and find some work.

Anything is better than continuing to live this depressing, humiliating life. I would rather die than continue to live in the same camp as Frederick.

I hate him. I'll show him. He'll regret treating me this way.

I swear on the power of the moon: I'll get even with Frederick if it's the last thing I do.

I did it, book. I'm so tired I might fall asleep as I write this.

Late last night, I snuck out of my wagon and made my way to Frederick's. Mama opened her eyes to look at me, but they were still distant.

She turned over and went back to sleep. Papa never stirred. He drank too much last night, and I slipped valerian root tincture into his drink when he wasn't looking.

The real risk was waking Frederick. I knew if he woke while I was taking his box, he'd be justified in using violence. But luck was with me. Frederick wasn't in his wagon. He must've gone off into the night as a wolf, even though the moon was at its lowest.

But he left the box. He left it right where he'd shown me. The fool. I snatched it up from under his bedding, threw it into my sack of food, and ran for the road.

I've never been so excited and so scared at the same time.

Now I'm hiding beneath the brush. I traveled all day. My bones hurt, and my stomach won't stop growling. But I need to be sparing with food. I don't know when I'll find the next town or when I'll find work. At least I'm free of that horrible camp.

A few nights on cold, hard ground will be worth it when I make my fortune.

 **4**

I RAN THROUGH THE woods, no light but that of the moon to guide me. I perked my ears to listen as I dodged trees and scurried over brush.

Family. Friends. The thoughts whirled inside my head. *Murder. Granny. If I run faster, it will all go away, it will all stop.* I pushed myself to pick up the speed.

For three days, I'd hidden in Drina's wagon by day and sat beside her fire at night. Three days of eating food with more flavor than any I'd ever eaten before. Three days of learning more about my mother than I had ever wanted to know.

A child of the stars married a child of the village - it could never end well. Drina's voice echoed in my head even as I ran faster through the woods.

Your mother was born of Frederick's line. She was raised within our people as a daughter of the stars. Your father came from a long line of the moon, but his family denied the power coursing through their veins. They assimilated and hid, longing to be a part of a way of life outside their destiny.

We tried to keep your parents apart. But love is not always wise. Your father's family left Fell Village when he married your mother. They knew it was only a matter of time before their lives would be destroyed.

My thoughts broke as I approached the village. I slowed my pace and came to a halt, listening for any guards or search parties that might still be out looking for me.

Nothing but the scamper of squirrels and fluttering of bats in trees met my ears. The village was asleep. *It's now or never.* I thought, debating whether I'd be safer in my wolf form or my human form. *Found in either one could get me killed instantly, but my hands would be more useful than my fangs for what I'm about to do.*

Slipping back into human form, I took a moment to catch my breath, then snatched up the clothes Drina had put in the sack draped around my neck and back. The cool air hit my skin, and I shivered as I pulled on my pants and shirt, missing the warmth of my wolf fur.

Nausea crept up, but I did as Drina had instructed and fixed my eyes on the moon, counting to ten as I took in three deep breaths. Soon, the nausea faded, and I stepped out from the cover of trees into the alleyway between the butcher and the baker.

The village continued in silence, the moon above lighting my way. I stuck to the shadows as I crept toward Granny's mill. I ducked behind a barrel just before three men marched by. They were all armed to the teeth.

"Where do you reckon he went then? Ain't seen any sign of the dog since that first night."

The skin on my neck prickled, and the urge to return to my wolf form surfaced, but I pushed it down and dug my fingers into the side of the barrel.

"As I see it, he's either run off like the coward he is, or," the man paused, as if ready to reveal some great secret. "Or he's lyin' in wait for us. Biding his time, he is. As soon as we let down our guard, he'll come runnin' to slash every one of our throats with his talons. Just like he done to Granny."

I shivered, the sudden urge to vomit washing over me as I considered what he'd said. To my relief, their footsteps receded, and I was left in silence once more. Creeping out from behind the barrel, I peered around the corner toward Granny's mill and checked for any guards.

The bright moonlight illuminated the empty streets. No one stood guard at the front of Granny's. Checking over my shoulder and around the houses one more time, I made a run for the shadows of the mill.

Sweat broke out over my forehead as I tried to calm my racing heart. *No one sounded the alarm. If they'd seen you, they would've woken the entire village. You're still safe. You're still undetected.* I leaned against the wall behind me and took a deep breath.

My heart stilled and the sweat began to disappear. *You're almost inside. Just a few more steps. If the door is locked, you go in through a window. And if there's someone inside, then we'll deal with that later.*

I tried not to think about who might be inside. The Travelers had heard through the grapevine that Red had been staying with a friend since her Granny died. *Who would want to stay in a death house?* I ignored the obvious answer of "me". I lived in the same house where they'd murdered my grandfather. *We're not thinking about that now. Only about getting inside the mill.*

After one more glance around, I turned the corner and walked toward the front door. My hand reached the doorknob and I turned it, pushing gently as I did. Incredulous relief flooded my mind as the door swung open without a sound, revealing nothing but a dark room inside.

Gathering my wits, I ducked through the door and closed it behind me. *Should I lock it?* I wondered, leaning back with relief as I listened for the presence of anyone inside. *Yes.* A ticking sounded off to the side. *A clock?* I guessed. The only place I'd ever seen a clock was inside the butcher's shop. Most people couldn't afford a luxury like that.

My eyes began to adjust to the dark, shapes of furniture and wall fixtures emerging in the filtered moonlight that drifted through the windows. I'd never been inside Granny's mill before. *Never been lucky enough to have any grain to mill.* I thought, my stomach growling at the thought of bread, even though Drina had fed me until I thought I would burst.

The room before me was large, stretching out and around an enormous fireplace that sat in the middle of the room. A ladder near the back led to the attic through a small hole in the wood beam ceiling. A small door sat in the opposite corner, leading out the back of the mill. *It must lead to the water wheel.* I surmised.

A majestic four-poster bed sat against the left wall, draped in thick curtains glinting red in the moonlight. My eyes drifted over the bed to the chaos surrounding it. A large stand lay on its side, its porcelain wash basin and bowl shattered on the floor.

To my right lay a couple of chairs, legs ripped apart and flung on the floor. A table next to the fireplace held a mess of spoiled food, the stench of it beginning to reach my nose as I continued to stare in horror.

Blood was everywhere. Dark stains of it covered every curtain and piece of furniture. It seemed as though blood had been splattered and wiped by the hand of a giant, pools of it all over the floor.

I was not prepared for this. I thought, exhaling slowly. *I don't know what I was expecting, but it wasn't this.*

I took a tentative step forward, taking care not to step on anything that looked wet. *The last thing I need to do is leave fresh footprints all over.* I walked toward the bed, alternating between a tiptoe and standing on one foot. Without thinking, I grabbed the first bedpost I came into contact with.

My hand withdrew of its own accord, and my stomach responded with horror. Deep grooves resembling claw marks had been etched into the inside of the bedpost. Dried blood came away with my hand, and a stench I'd never known before hit my nostrils. I became increasingly grateful that I could only see what the sparse moonlight allowed.

Focus. What are you looking for? Closing my eyes, I took a deep breath, opened my eyes, and looked around. More claw marks met my gaze, just barely visible in the dark room, but I knew the fact that I could still see them meant they were deep. My heart sank.

No wonder they all believe it was you. Blood everywhere, claw marks all over the furniture and walls, and the victim is the one who took the life of your grandfather. Is it any wonder they believe so sincerely it was you?

I took a few tentative steps toward the fireplace and the table of spoiled food. *More blood spatter.* My eyes surveyed the meat, bugs crawling on the stale bread. White cheese contrasted with the blood spatter.

Who did this? I wondered, frowning as I realized that I'd been set up. *And why are there three place settings?* My frown deepened as I continued to look at the table. Three plates, all dirty, sat on the table. *And where was Red when the killing took place?*

The questions were beginning to overwhelm my brain. I rubbed the bridge of my nose. *I came here to find answers. What if I blacked out and did this without realizing it?* The idea terrified me. *What if I'm guilty after all? No one else in the village has my...curse.* I'd posed the possibility to Drina only hours before.

"No one else *that you know of* has your abilities." She'd said, tilting her head to one side with a soft smile on her lips. *Abilities. Not curse. Abilities.* She'd been very specific in her wording. "In all of our history as children of the Stars and the Moon, none of us has ever committed a crime and not remembered it the next day. That is a lie touted by those who would have us exterminated for no other reason than they fear our powers."

Shaking my head out of my reverie, I looked around as a sense of defeat swelled inside my chest. *I don't know what to do or where to look.* I thought, tears burning at the edges of my eyes. *Maybe the best thing I can do is leave for good. Let them all believe what they want to believe.* Clenching my hands into fists, I wished I could punch someone.

But I didn't do it. Some small voice kept repeating to me. *It wasn't me. Why should I be blamed? Why should I pay for the crime of another?* My mother's face flashed before my eyes, her jaw set in response to me asking her why I was being judged for the crimes of my grandfather.

Were they even his crimes to begin with? The question made me blink in surprise. *I didn't do this, but either someone who can transform committed this murder, or they knew how to make it look like I'd done it.* I shook my head, still blinking. *Is it so hard to assume that my grandfather might also have been framed?*

A rattling of the door startled me out of my reverie. *Someone's coming.* I glanced around in horror. The blood pulsated in my neck as I tried to contain the wolf longing to come out. *Hide. Anywhere. It doesn't matter.*

Without another thought, I took a few swift strides toward the bed and crawled underneath, pulling the cover that hung over the side a few inches further toward the floor. Seconds after I pulled the cover down, the back door flew open, hitting the wall with a bang.

I held my breath and waited, hoping against all odds that whoever it was wouldn't look under the bed. Heavy footsteps entered the room. *They didn't close the back door behind them.* I realized. It could only mean one thing. *They're not afraid of being caught. Who is this?*

A cold sweat broke out on my forehead as my curiosity blossomed. I peered out from beneath the bedframe, holding my breath. Large boots came into view as the man walked through the moonlight scattered about the floor. Slow, methodical steps took him away from my view as I shrank beneath the bed, wondering if my heartbeat was as loud to him as it was to me.

Plates moved, chairs scraped, and things I couldn't guess at were thrown to the floor. *What is he doing?* I wondered, my mind racing with possibilities. *Is he looking for clues? Why look in the wee hours of the morning? Why now and not a few days ago?* I listened as more of Granny's belongings tumbled to the floor. *Because he can't look during the day any more than you can, dummy.* I closed my eyes as my heart rate spiked again.

"Damn it all to hell." The man muttered. *That voice is familiar.* I thought, trying to place it. *It's someone in town.* I was about to creep closer to the edge of the bedframe and take a chance at looking out when I heard new footsteps approaching. Soft and light, they crept in from the back door and stood just within view.

Red. I thought, blinking as I considered the well-known red leather ankle boots I'd seen a hundred times before. *No one else has boots quite like them. No one else deserves boots the color of courage.* A chill ran down my spine, and I had to keep from letting out the air I was holding in.

"The sun is about to come up," Red said, her voice barely above a whisper. "Did you find them?" Fear enveloped every word she uttered.

"No." The man bit out, his voice harsh but quiet. *Who is that?* I racked my brain for a match to the voice. I'd spent so little time speaking with the inhabitants of Fell.

"The old lady must've burnt them all or buried them." The distinct sound of knuckles cracking met my ears. "That is, unless you're lying to me, and you know where she hid them." My mouth went dry as I listened to him take a few steps until he stood toe-to-toe with Red. "You wouldn't lie to me now, would you, Red?"

"No." Red's voice shook as she spoke, her feet unmoving. "I swear, I don't know where she put them. I didn't even know they existed."

Tense silence filled the mill. I waited, wondering if they'd be able to hear my breathing as I urged myself to ignore the cramp in my left calf.

"Well then," the man's rough voice broke the silence like a boulder grating along a dirt road. "I suppose that's good news for you." He pushed past Red without another word, exiting through the back door.

Red let out a shaky sigh, then turned and followed suit, shutting the back door behind her.

I gasped for air.

70 years Earlier
Celeste, 13

Spring

I met a farmer on the road a few days after I ran away. He asked me where I'd come from. I cried and told him my family had abandoned me.

Out of pity, he gave me a ride to his farm, a hot meal at his table, and a few nights in his barn in exchange for some cleaning.

His wife died this winter, and he and his son have no idea how to do their own laundry. I made a deal with him and stayed a couple of weeks. He paid me in shelter, food, and a few coins.

But I want more than that. I knew if I stayed, I'd end up stuck forever. He would force me to marry him or his son. I'll never let another man force me to do something I don't want to. I left in the middle of the night last night. Took his horse and a sack of cheese and cured meat with me. By the time he would have noticed this morning, I was long gone.

The fool.

I have no idea where I'm headed, but if I keep following this road, I should find a village or even a citadel. If everything goes according to plan, I'll make my fortune. I can't do that if I'm working for a stupid farmer.

I made it to a small citadel, book. The people are gruff and dirty, and rude. But they pay well for laundry and a hot meal. The local innkeeper hired me five minutes after he met me. He's paying me less than I deserve, but I needed a place to board my horse and a place to sleep.

The men who stay here are merchants. They sail in from faraway places with tales of the sea. I love to listen to their exaggerated tales of mythical creatures and pirates.

The more I flirt with them, the more money I make. As if I'd ever consider letting them touch me. All I want is their coin. I've been keeping it in the box. It took me a few tries, but I figured out how to open it.

Now I keep it all in there underneath a floorboard beneath my bed. Someday I'll find a shifter again, one who loves me in return. I can use the box on him so that he's bound to me forever. Frederick will regret his decision; he'll regret laughing at me.

5

I'M NOT SURE HOW long I lay beneath the bed, shaking and gasping for breath. By the time my body stopped shaking and exhaustion crept in, I realized morning light would soon arrive. *I must leave this mill before the sun comes up.* I thought, crawling my way back out.

I surveyed the mess - an even bigger mess than when I'd arrived. The man hadn't bothered to watch his footprints, but I didn't see any that resembled Red's. *What were they looking for?* I searched the broken plates, the scattered food, and the bloody footprints.

The glow of the waning moonlight caught my attention, and my eyes drifted to the fireplace. I squinted, pushing myself up to my feet to walk over. *Is that brick out of place?* I reached out, hesitant to touch said brick. *Or is the mortar a different color?*

As I pushed on it, the brick moved ever so slightly. With trembling fingers, I grabbed a knife off the table to pry at the mortar around it. *It's not mortar, it's mud.* I realized as it crumbled easily beneath the pressure of the blade in my hand.

Wiggling the loosened brick back and forth, I pulled it from its spot and peered into the hole. My heart raced as my eyes fell on a thin wooden box. Reaching in, I cursed as my knuckles scraped against the brick. Gritting my teeth, I pulled the box out.

Angling the box in the moonlight, I gaped at the carved design staring back at me from the lid. A wolf howling at the moon had been expertly etched into the light-colored oak, the grooves stained dark to accent the design.

Ignoring the blood smearing from my knuckles onto the box, I flipped it on its side. My fingers ran across the carving of an axe. I turned it around, following what looked like claw marks around the remaining sides. *Who was Granny?* I stared, my mind racing as I realized she was not the person I'd been raised to think she was.

Fumbling at the lid, I pulled, but nothing happened. Turning it over in my hands, I wondered if I had it upside down. But to no avail. Holding it up to my ear, I shook it, wondering if it wasn't a box but rather some kind of decoration. *Something is in there.* I confirmed, standing there staring at it as I considered what to do.

Voices outside brought me out of my reverie. *Get out of this mill and go back to the Travelers.* I thought, cursing under my breath. I tucked the box under my arm, picked up the loose brick, and returned it to its spot. *Doesn't look the same without the mud, but at least it's not a gaping hole.*

I considered going out the back door, much as Red and her companion had. However, considering they might both be out there, I decided against the idea and crept toward the front door. Cracking it open and glancing around, I checked for the passing guards. Nothing stirred.

I left the mill quickly, shutting the door behind me and darting through the shadows again. One glance at the faint rays of pink in the sky showed me how long I'd been there and how foolish I was. *You could've been caught at the scene of the crime. They would've hung you right then and there. After all, what other proof would any of them require?*

I reached the tree line of the woods and took off at a sprint, the box clutched in my left hand. Racing back to Drina, hopeful she might know how to open the box. Hopeful it might give me answers to the ever-growing list of questions.

I didn't stop running until I reached the Traveler's clearing. The sun had begun to peek over the tops of the trees, brightening the circle of wagons. Stopping short at the circle, I leaned against the nearest wagon to catch my breath.

Morning fires were being lit, the youngest children were running around together, and the smell of breakfast permeated the air. My breathing slowed as a sense of calm settled over me. *I may not have answers yet. I may have more questions than answers. But I'm safe. If only for a little while.*

Searching the circle for Drina's wagon, I found it at the opposite end. Her rounded, forest-green canopy was draped in colorful scarves and dried branches. Lanterns hung at the doorway, a red woven blanket falling across it. *Like a tent on wheels with a hard floor.* I thought.

Drina herself stood over a fire, stirring a pot. Her thick black hair had been gathered into a braid that fell to her waist, the adornments of feathers and dried flowers rearranged to fit the hairstyle. She looked up as I approached, eyes seeming to pierce through my very soul.

"You're back." She announced to herself as she searched my face. "What did you find?" She straightened and held out her hand. Without hesitation, I placed the box in her upturned palm.

"I couldn't open it," I said, watching as she turned it over in her hands.

"Is this your blood?" She asked, looking over at me with concern. "Or did someone attack you?" I held up my right hand, the bloodied knuckles now scabbing over. She nodded in understanding and returned to her examination of the box.

"It's a puzzle box." She stated, offering it back to me. "You'll have to figure out how it opens, or," she hesitated, resisting as I tried to take it back. "Or you'll have to risk damaging whatever is inside and smash it open with a rock." Her eyes locked in on the carving of the wolf. "That would be a shame." Releasing the box, she looked at me with anticipation, as if awaiting my decision.

I stared at the howling wolf. "I don't want to destroy it." I said. "I'll try to figure out how it opens. Have you seen a box like this before?" I looked up at her, hopeful.

She nodded. "Once." She said, frowning as her eyes glazed over. "A very long time ago, when I was a child, a box just like that one was carved from an oak that fell during a storm."

"A box like this one? Or this box?" I asked, turning it over again in my hands.

Drina shrugged. "Who can say? I believe it to be one and the same. However," she went back to stirring the pot over the fire. "It is difficult to be sure."

"What happened to the box?"

"It was stolen. Taken in the middle of the night by one of our own. Never to be seen again. Not the box nor the child who took it."

I blinked. "Was the child a girl?" I asked, my voice quiet as I waited for the answer I already knew.

"Yes."

My pulse raced. "Might that girl have grown up to be an old woman who ran a mill in Fell Village?" I asked.

"Yes," Drina repeated.

"Why did she take the box?" I asked, shaking my head. "Does it possess some secret power I can't see on the surface?" I ran my thumb over the carving of the wolf, tracing the outline as I processed the information I'd been given.

"You're asking all the right questions except for one," Drina said, never pausing as she continued to stir.

I felt her eyes on me and looked up to meet her gaze. "What's that?"

"You have not asked me who carved the box."

My mouth went dry. "Who carved the box?" I whispered, horror sweeping over me.

"Your grandfather." We stared at one another. "He was barely fifteen when he carved the box." She continued. "I remember watching him from my wagon while my mother cooked our meals. He cut away the most desirable part of the tree, brought it back to his wagon, and spent the next three days carving what I believe you hold in your hands now.

"He was a talented young wolf. All the young Travelers looked up to him as their leader. The only thing I do not know, and can only suspect, is whether he poured any kind of magic into the box as he created it."

Magic. Puzzle boxes. My grandfather. My fingers tightened on the box as unexpected anger surged inside me. "Then, I suppose this box belongs to me now," I said, clenching my jaw as I spoke. "It was stolen, but not by me."

Drina held my gaze and nodded.

"How old was the girl who stole the box?" I asked, still piecing things together.

"She could not have been more than thirteen."

"Was she, that is..." My mouth went dry again as I became unsure of how to ask my question.

"You want to know if she was also a talented young Traveler." Drina guessed, returning her gaze to the food. "That depends on your definition, I suppose. She had not, as far as I know, shown herself to be a wolf. But that does not mean she couldn't wield the power of the stars."

I nodded, suddenly fatigued and wishing I could lie down and sleep for a long while.

"Sit, child," Drina said, startling me out of my reverie. "You need rest and food. The box will wait another few hours."

I nodded and sat before the fire, still holding the box in my hands.

"Why?" I whispered, shaking my head. "Why steal this box? Why run away? Why do I always find more questions when I'm trying to uncover the answers?"

"Ah, child. Answers are rarely what we hope them to be." Drina stooped to pick up a bowl before spooning a large portion of food into it and offering it to me. "However," she continued. "I do have a few more answers for you."

Setting down the box in front of my feet, I took the breakfast offered to me. Steam curled up to lick my face as I took in the scent of spiced apples and sweet potato mash. I'd grown cold without realizing it, and my fingers tingled at the warmth in the bowl.

"Your grandfather and Red's granny go back much farther than you've been led to believe. Some say they were sweethearts." I looked up at Drina in alarm. She smiled and held up a hand as if to calm me. "Others, like myself, believe that Granny fancied your grandfather and her attention was not returned."

My body relaxed as the disturbing idea of Red being a distant relative of mine drifted away. "So," I ventured, stirring the food absentmindedly. "She took the box out of spite. But why? What's so important about this box?" My eyes drifted to the box sitting on the ground.

Taking a bite of food, my mouth exploded with flavor. I savored the bite before swallowing. "Did she live in the village when she ran away? The Travelers would have found her and brought her home if she'd only gone to the village." Frowning, I looked up at her, hoping she knew at least a few more answers.

Drina shook her head as she sat down on the opposite side of the fire, a bowl of food in her own hands. "No," she said. "I believe she ran off to places far from here. As you said, we would have found her and brought her back if she'd only fled as far as the village." She took a bite, her sharp eyes closing in enjoyment.

"Besides," she said, licking her lips as her hand poised with another spoonful of food. "Fell Village was but a thought when Granny was a child. A few scattered houses around a well. There was nothing there for a young girl trying to..." Drina's voice faltered as she tilted her head, thinking. "Trying to do whatever it was she was trying to do." She laughed, shrugging her shoulders.

We ate in silence for a few minutes. I devoured my breakfast, my mind racing as my stomach responded to the food.

"Why did she hate my grandfather so much? So much that she came back to ruin his life." The bitterness in my voice was unavoidable.

"I don't know why she came back," Drina said, hesitating.

"What is it? You do know something." I urged, setting my empty bowl down to pick up the box again. "Please, it might help me solve how to open this box."

She shook her head and shrugged, staring at the box. "It's just," her eyes drifted to meet mine. "Your grandfather was never seen changing into his wolf form again after Granny left. That is, after the box was stolen."

I almost dropped the box in shock and horror. "You mean," I stuttered, unable to tear my eyes away from hers. "The box has something to do with my grandfather's powers?"

Drina nodded. "That is my belief. Until we open it, we cannot know for certain."

"Then let's get it open," I said, my heart racing with anticipation.

65 years Earlier
Celeste, 18

Summer

A young man came into the inn today. Fresh from the countryside. He's tall, with black hair that falls below his shoulders and a body I can get used to. His clothes were rough and homespun, his boots nearly worn through the toe. He may be a farmer, but one look at his black eyes and I knew he's also a son of the moon. A few smiles, one free drink, and the poor man spilled his life story to me.

His name's Evan. He inherited his ability to shift from his father. They quarreled, and Evan left yesterday, forbidden from ever returning.

He said he's tired of living by the rules of another. He wants to make his way in the world, not just shift into a wolf to keep the livestock safe from wild animals.

I told him where I came from, how I want to change the trajectory of my life. We talked late into the night, even after the innkeeper went to bed. I think Evan may be the right one. I've been here for over five years, waiting for the right person to come along. I've met other shifters, but none were ready to follow me or fall in love with me.

Maybe I can convince Evan to try out the box. It all depends on how I spin the idea.

Love. Infatuation. Devotion. It's the only way. Evan needs to be head over heels in love with me before I spring the idea on him. This won't be hard. The poor man has been starved of all physical affection. I see the way he looks at me. This is the right time.

It's been three months. Evan adores me. Every night he spends with me, he wakes with a smile on his face. Last week I asked him to shift for me. He did so, willingly showing me how he can shift. Each night since, I've asked him to do the same. He does without question, his face lighting up with every compliment I give after he shifts back to his human form.

Tonight we're going to the woods. It's the full moon, and he wants to show me what it's like to shift beneath the full moon. I'll pretend I've never seen such a thing.

My plan is working. My heart is full, I and his power is within my reach. I will ask for his blood as a sign of his devotion soon. I'll show him the box, explain how trust can mold our relationship. I believe he will agree.

6

FOR THE NEXT HOUR, Drina and I turned the box over in our hands, pushing each side and corner every which way we could imagine. Sometimes things would click, the sounds of gears shifting or a piece of wood moving. Sometimes nothing happened at all.

"Do you think it opens in sequence, or can it open out of sequence, and we're getting stuck because of that?" I asked, frustration growing in my chest.

Drina shook her head, taking the box from me to flip over once more. "If there's one thing I remember about your grandfather," she started, squinting and nudging the left-hand side of the box. "It's that he had a love of method and logic. I don't believe he would have designed a box that would open out of sequence."

A new piece slid open from the right side as she spoke, and she pulled it out as far as it would go, testing to see if it would turn to the left or the right. It turned clockwise. My heart raced as Drina returned the box to me. Wordlessly, I continued to push.

Suddenly, it was like an avalanche. With each push, a new, small piece would jut out, allowing us to push and pull and turn something else. The box looked crazy. A small drawer popped out with a click. I pulled and found a silver key. Dumping it out into my hand, I held the key up for Drina to see.

"Where?" I asked, unable to form a complete sentence. She took the box after staring at the key and turned it over again. Nothing happened as she poked and prodded.

"Maybe..." She mumbled, her eyes focusing on the drawer jutting out from the bottom of the box. She pulled it a little harder, and it came out completely. Flipping it upside down, she revealed a keyhole.

"You do the honors, child," she said, excitement shining in her eyes as she handed the box back to me. "Your grandfather created this masterpiece. You deserve to be the one who opens it."

Without another word, I inserted the key and turned it a full circle. A small click sounded at the top of the box, and the carved part slid forward. Leaving the key inserted, I nudged the lid forward a little further before pushing it up. It slid with ease, still attached on the far end as it opened upwards for me to look inside.

At the bottom of the box sat a small stack of yellowed letters with broken wax seals. I stared at them in disbelief before looking up at Drina. The pulse in my neck raced as she nodded at me to pick them up. Gingerly, I drew out the top letter between two fingers and placed it in my left hand to stare at the wax seal.

The tiniest imprint of a hand holding stars looked back at me from the folded, faded paper. "Is this a seal you've seen before?" I asked Drina without looking up.

"Our people are not in the habit of sending or sealing letters," Drina replied. Confusion consumed her words. "Our communities are few, and we rarely exchange information that can be used against us or stolen." She reached out to trace the seal with her index finger before pulling her hand hastily away. I looked up at her frowning face.

"Read it, child. Pay no attention to the ramblings of an old woman." She said, trying to force a smile as she rubbed her finger with her thumb.

After a second's hesitation, I opened the paper to reveal neat, intricate writing. The paper was not much bigger than the width of both my hands. I read aloud.

Evan,

If you look to the right as you climb the great hill toward the manor, you'll see a small gap in the fence. Be sure you maintain your human form both entering and leaving the property, as your wolf form will not fit through such a thin gap.

Follow the flower beds inside toward the side of the manor. I will leave the side window unlocked. Close it as you leave, and I will lock it when I go back into work in the morning.

The Processor has promised a generous reward on top of the sum already paid if you can contain the execution to the bedroom. In other words: do not allow the lord to escape. Be silent, be quick, and make a good show of it.

Don't forget the necklace. He keeps it in a small box in a false bottom of his bedside table drawer.

I will meet you at the tree beneath the moonlight.

–Celeste

I paused, staring at what I'd just read. "Was that Granny's name?" I asked, realizing I'd never heard her called by anything else.

"I don't remember," Drina said, her voice quiet as she reached out for the letter. Handing it to her, I took up the next in the small stack still inside the box. The same broken wax seal was on this letter.

"Go on," Drina said, nodding. "Keep reading."

Evan,

The Processor has a new job for us. Meet me at the tree beneath the moonlight tomorrow night. There's a farmer to the south who refuses to bend the knee. Your target is his daughter. I'll lead you to the farm and show you where she sleeps. You'll take it from there.

He was pleased with your work at the manor. A few more jobs, and we will never want for anything ever again.

–Celeste

"Who was Evan?" I asked, not even pausing. "Is he still alive?" I looked up at Drina. She was squinting her eyes, staring at the letter in my hand like she was looking for something secret.

"There's a sort of idea brewing in my head – a memory long forgotten," she said, a slight frown forming. "I believe Granny's husband was named Evan." Drina frowned, her eyes going distant as she continued to stare at me.

I blinked at her in disbelief. "You mean the two of them were hired assassins before they came to live in Fell Village, running a mill?" I was incredulous. *Who would give up a life of wealth and adventure to settle in a miserable little village that barters with others for food and supplies not readily available nearby?*

"Read the rest," she said, gesturing toward the unread letters with her chin. "The answer might come to us."

I nodded, handed her the letter, and scooped out the rest. Only three remained.

Evan,

Someone saw us at the tree beneath the moonlight. The only way forward, the only way to save ourselves, is to silence them before they expose us. I know their face. I tracked them back to the village inn. I fear they were hired to track us. I know not by who.

The Processor will come after us if we don't take care of the problem. He's made it clear that our fate is tied to the success of this mission.

Meet me in the field behind the manor beside the sunflower patch. As always, beneath the moonlight.

–Celeste

I handed the letter to Drina and opened the next without a word.

Evan,

The Processor is pleased with the success of our last mission. He has high hopes of no one else bothering us.

We have a new target. The farmer continues to defy The Processor. We've been instructed to take out the rest of his family. The Processor will take possession of his farm soon after. The goal is to stop the spread before a full-on infection takes hold.

Meet me at the edge of the farm beneath the moonlight. I will assist you in person in this mission. Bring your axe.

–Celeste

The last letter was different. I paused as I went to open it. No seal, dark paper like that you would find in a butcher's shop to wrap meat. I showed it to Drina. She nodded in understanding as I opened it to read. Scrawling handwriting met my gaze, messy and crooked. The paper was stained with grease.

I will find you.

No matter where you go, no matter how you try to hide, I will find you.

Consider this my solemn vow. Until the day I die, I will hunt you down.

With my last breath, I will seek your demise.

Witch and Wolf, bitch and bastard, I will destroy your lives until your lungs can no longer draw breath.

The Processor begged for his life before I took it.

You will beg for death before I'm through with you.

I blinked, re-reading the letter silently. No names, no indication of when the letter was sent or received. Drina let out a slow breath and I looked up.

"Let me hold the letter." She said, her face drawn. I handed it to her. She paused, closing her eyes as the paper balanced in her palm.

"I see the face of a man, large and burly, with red hair, a thick beard, and a meat cleaver in his hands." She nodded, closing her fingers around the letter. "I've never met him before, never seen his face in my travels. Does that fit the description of anyone in Fell?" She asked, opening her eyes to meet my gaze.

I did a mental check of all the people I could remember from the village - starting with the local butcher. But I came up empty-handed. "Burly men live in the village. But none with red hair." I shrugged. "The butcher is a slight man with black hair and beady eyes. While I wouldn't care to cross him," I laughed nervously. "I also wouldn't fear him."

We sat in silence for a moment, each lost in our thoughts.

"None of this makes any sense," I said, despair and exhaustion washing over me. "Why did she steal the box? Who is Evan? Who is The Processor? Who is this man that vowed to kill them?" I buried my head in my hands. "And what in all the names of the stars does any of this have to do with my grandfather and Granny's desire to ruin our lives?"

Drina didn't reply. My body ached, longing for sleep. Pushing myself to my feet, I bent down and picked up the box. As I brought it up, something clattered around inside it. I stopped and peered inside, tilting it back and forth.

A small vial rolled across the bottom from underneath the lip of the lid. I tipped the box over, and the vial landed in my hand. Gasping, I turned to show Drina.

"Is that..." My voice disappeared as we both stared. Drina rose to her feet, shock on her face.

"Blood." She whispered. "That's a vial of blood."

We continued to stare at the vial of blood without speaking. Drina held out her hand for me to drop it in her palm. I did, reluctantly.

"Why would Granny have a vial of blood?" I asked.

"The real question is whose blood did she have?" Drina responded, turning it over in her hand to hold up between her index finger and thumb. Sunlight glinted through the upper, empty portion of the round vial. The smallest cork I'd ever seen stopped it at the top.

My whole body sagged with exhaustion as we stood there, still staring at the vial. "What do we do now?" I asked, unable to contain the weariness in my voice.

Drina turned to look at me. "We don't do anything right now. *You* go to sleep. Just as we planned before this fell out of that strange box." She tucked the vial into her belt and patted it with her hand.

"This isn't going anywhere. I need time to think, to ask questions. My instincts tell me there's a magic attached to this box and its contents that I've never seen before." Her eyes glossed over as she spoke.

"Now," her eyes snapped back to focus on me, looking me up and down with concern. "Go rest. You just regained your strength, child. I won't have you getting sick all over again. When you wake, we'll speak again."

I nodded, too tired to argue. Unsure of what I would say if I did try to argue. I stepped up into her wagon, taking the box with me, and collapsed into the luxurious blankets and cushions.

My brain soon stilled, and sleep overtook me. My dreams were haunted by visions of the letters I'd read. Blood-spattered rooms of a mansion and a farm played before my closed eyes as I slept. An unknown face turned from man to wolf as I searched for the tree where a younger Granny was waiting beneath the moonlight.

The box with its carved lid of a wolf came back to my dream-filled eyes on repeat. The grooves shone beneath the moonlight, the vial of blood on constant replay. *The blood must be spilled in the grooves of the lid.* A man's voice whispered in my dreams. *Spill the blood in the grooves of the lid.*

65 years Earlier
Celeste, 18

<u>Summer</u>

Last night, Evan gave me a vial of his blood as a sign of his devotion and love for me. I showed him the box, explaining the "myth" I'd heard surrounding it. His eyes lit up with curiosity. He wanted to try it.

One drop of his blood in the carving of the box, and he fell under my control. The power flowed through my hands, each beat of his heart as he ran through the forest. Our minds melded as one. Everything he saw, I witnessed as well. Everything he thought, I heard. Everything I wanted him to do, he obeyed without question.

When he changed back to his human form, he agreed that the box is a great test of our loyalty and devotion to each other. He swore on his life to protect me - to protect our secret. Then he gave me his blood to keep as a sign of his trust in me.

I've locked the vial inside the box.

Evan is mine.

7

I SLEPT FOR HOURS, waking slightly as Drina came in to sleep on her pad, but drifting back to sleep immediately. I woke at dawn the next day, hunger and thirst too strong to remain asleep. Drina's heavy breathing continued as I pushed myself up and crawled out of the wagon. I left the box behind.

The sun was peaking over the trees, vivid rays of pink and gold casting their spell on a foggy clearing. The crisp air hit my cheeks, and I blinked, feeling more alert. After drinking my fill of water from the jug strapped to the wagon, I dug through Drina's stash for a chunk of bread and an apple. Stirring up the fire, I added wood and sat down beside it.

I contemplated the events of the last few days as I bit into my apple, the sweet tartness a welcome offset to the stale bread. The words of my dream came back to me as I chewed my apple.

Spill the blood in the grooves of the lid. I frowned. *What will happen? How is this not something Drina thought to do?* As though hearing my thoughts, Drina pulled the door curtain aside and stepped out.

Her eyes went from the crackling fire to me sitting beside it.

"The blood," I said, swallowing the last piece of apple in my mouth and setting the core down beside the fire. "I think I know what to do with it."

Drina paused to stare at me in disbelief, turned back into the wagon, then emerged a moment later with the box in hand. She sat beside me, handing over the box as she withdrew the vial of blood from the safety of her belt.

"I believe we have the same idea," she said, her hand hovering over the box as I held it in my almost shaking hands. "But I must warn you, I don't know what will happen." She frowned, uncorking the vial. "I cannot promise your safety."

Nodding, I moved the box in her direction. Holding my breath, I watched as she tipped the vial over and allowed three drops of blood to flood the crevices of the lid. We both waited, staring as the blood moved through the design.

Seconds ticked by. Nothing happened.

I released the breath inside my lungs, unsure of what I'd expected to happen, slightly disappointed that nothing had happened.

"Now what?" I asked, glancing up at Drina as I kept the box steady. Drina continued to watch the box, her eyes tracing the red pool of a wolf. "Does this mean that's not the reason for the blood?"

"The letters always maintained that they met beneath the moonlight," Drina's voice was pensive as she tilted her head to one side. "Even after the tree was no longer a safe place to meet, they always met beneath the moonlight." Finally, she met my stare. "Which means we try again under the moonlight."

I nodded, my pulse racing at the thought.

"Until then," Drina continued, corking the vial and returning it to her belt with another gentle pat. "I suggest you pour out those drops into the fire and allow the sun to bleach away the residue.

I did as she commanded, the blood hissing as it hit the fire. As the sun came over the trees, I climbed up to the roof of the wagon and placed the box where none could see it but the orb of light above. By the time I came back to the fire, Drina had breakfast brewing.

We ate in companionable silence. Stale bread, stewed apples in cream, and a mug of hot tea with sugar. The apples were bursting with flavor, sweet and tart and spiced to perfection. *I haven't eaten like this since...* My thoughts dragged off as I tried to remember when I'd enjoyed such a simple but delicious meal. *Who am I trying to fool? Myself? I've never eaten like this. Even before Mama died.* The thought sobered me.

As soon as we finished eating, Drina waved me away. "There's nothing for you to do right now," she said, gathering our bowls and mugs to wash. "Go look for mushrooms for supper. I have a hunk of cured meat and a stash of vegetables I need to use up."

She waved me away again. "Off with you. Find me some mushrooms. But don't wander too far or for too long, child." She smiled at me, then turned away with another wave of her hand.

Grabbing a linen sack hanging inside the wagon, I strapped a knife to my waist, shouldered my bow and arrows, threw on my cloak, and trudged off into the woods. While the sunshine was warm, the dense trees of the forest held onto the fall chill in the shade of their branches.

I wandered through the quiet forest for hours, ducking to gather mushrooms wherever I found them, tucking wild rosemary and lemon balm into my bag as well. *The cold will claim them if I don't.* I thought, crouching down to cut more sprigs of rosemary.

"Red!" The voice I'd heard in Granny's mill broke through the silence of the forest. "Stop!" I froze, my hands poised over the rosemary as I tried to decide what to do. *Where do I go?* I thought, glancing around to see where the voice was coming from.

"I can't do this anymore." Red's voice reached me, faint, but still there. "What do you want from me?" The desperation in her voice was obvious. "I've done everything you asked. Everything you both asked all my life," she was crying, notes of anger in her voice. "Now look where it's gotten me!"

I looked around for a shrub to hide under as the voices drew closer. Without a second to lose, I ran five feet and dove into the thick brush nearby. Branches scratched at my cheeks and tore my cloak. I bit back the urge to moan in pain as a red cloak emerged from the trees beside the rosemary I'd been about to cut.

I held my breath. *Always holding my breath. Every time they're near.* I thought, trying to make myself relax and listen.

"Let me go!" Red cried as the man grabbed her by the arms and shook. My heartbeat quickened. I wasn't sure if it was indignant rage that someone would grab another person like that or excitement that Granny's offspring was paying a price of cruelty I'd paid all my life.

"Shut up!" He growled at her, shaking her until I was sure her teeth would fall out of her mouth. The man wore a dark green cloak with an axe strapped across his back, his hood drawn up over his face.

Red's hood had long since fallen back over her shoulders. Messy brown braids drifted down her back. A tear-stained, freckled face was the only thing visible above her red cloak. Eyes so green and so full of fear, I wondered that I'd never noticed before.

Because you never dared look at her before. I realized. *Every time you saw her, you were in town. You couldn't look at her without the fear of someone hurting you and accusing you of something dreadful.*

"Listen here, girl." The man hissed, his hooded face inches from hers as he clenched her arms with his hands. "Everyone in that gods-forsaken village believes Wolf did it. If you're smart and want what's good for you, you'll let them continue to believe that." He squeezed, and Red whimpered, shrinking slightly as she tried to pull away.

"I won't take the fall for this. I won't go to the gallows for the death of that conniving, evil old woman." He shook Red again. "Do you understand? I won't give up my life so that some filthy, cursed boy can live." He let her go, pushing her away from himself.

"I did you and the world a favor. You know it. I know it. But I'll be damned if I let you ruin my life the way your Granny ruined mine and my father's, and his father before mine."

Red shrank from the man, massaging her right arm with her left hand, tears streaming down her face. I studied the man, willing him to remove the hood of his cloak. As if obeying my silent command, he pushed it back from his face. I blinked in disbelief, watching as the bearded woodcutter took a step toward Red. His pale skin was pink with fury, a sharp contrast to his black hair and eyes.

"You keep your mouth shut. You thank me and move on with your life," he said, jabbing the air between them with his right index finger. "The old hag deserved what happened to her. You of all people should know that."

What does that mean? I wondered, trying to ignore the cramp in my leg. I gritted my teeth against it and forced myself to remain still.

"But Fletcher –" Red tried to interject. *Fletcher.* I thought, watching as he took a step closer, his right hand raising as if to strike. *I know his face. But how?* Red cowered in front of him, holding up both hands as though they'd offer some shred of protection.

"If you breathe a word of what really happened to anyone, I will hunt you down and make sure you face the same fate as your Granny." He lowered his hand and took another step closer before grabbing her jaw and yanking it to force her to look him in the eye. "Do we understand one another?"

Red visibly gulped before nodding. Fletcher continued to stare at her for a few more seconds before yanking his hand away.

"Good." He said, brushing himself off and straightening his cloak. His eyes roamed the forest around them. I held my breath again, hoping the shade of the trees and my cloak would keep me from his practiced eyesight. His eyes passed over me quickly, not even pausing.

"I'll hear no more about this." He said, turning away from her. "Stay with your friends. Keep your mouth shut. Let the village hunt down that menace and hang him for her death." He took a step away and turned to face her one last time. "Then thank me as you live your life free from the monsters both within the village and without." He disappeared into the trees.

I was too shocked to be offended by words I'd been called my entire life. I turned back to watch Red. Her shoulders slumped, and she wiped a sleeve across her nose as she continued to cry.

"I hate you," Red muttered. To my amazement, she turned her face toward the sky and screamed the same words. "I hate you, Granny!" Her fear mingled with fury as she sank to her knees and sobbed.

For the first time in my life, I felt sorry for Red, the chosen child of Fell Village.

Autumn

We've been practicing. I started with once a week, at the change of the moon in the middle of the night. At first, Evan was reluctant, but I always reward him with something he'll enjoy. Lately, he's become more obedient. Like a trained pet at my side.

I chose well. I encourage him with thoughts of what we can accomplish together, how our dreams can come true. At times, I sense his doubt and fear. But I quickly distract him.

I've been adding in more practice times now. He said he misses changing into his wolf form, asking if I could release him so he can do it on his own, but keep his blood. I cried when he said that, sobbing about the way I thought our trust was deeper. It worked like a charm. He apologized and hasn't asked since. But I'll gladly give him more time to change.

The more he obeys, the better our communication becomes.

We've been practicing for months. I convinced Evan to begin our work. I contacted the sheriff in our citadel, asking him what criminals he needs caught. He laughed at me, told me I was a fool, but he gave me the information.

Tonight we practice catching criminals. The reward is small, but it's a chance to begin our work to secure our fortune. Evan is nervous, but excited. I can sense his resentment growing that I control his powers. But he can't escape me, and he knows I'll be devastated if he tries to ask for his freedom.

8

I WATCHED RED CRY for a few minutes, contemplating my next move. *I could wait until she leaves, then return to camp and tell Drina about it all. See what she thinks.* But the longer I waited, the less appealing that option became. *Or I could confront Red now and ask her to help me.* The idea made my pulse race with anticipation.

Why would she want to help me? Some part of my brain argued. *She's never helped me before. Why now?* I considered everything I'd witnessed. *Because she has a conscience, if that conversation is anything to go by. Because maybe she doesn't want to perpetuate the lies of Granny. It's worth a shot. She can't hurt me here.*

Without another moment to spend hesitating, I crawled out from the brush where I'd been hiding. Red gasped and fell backwards when she spotted me, scrambling to her feet to face me.

"I don't want to hurt you," I said, holding up both hands, one still grasping the bag of mushrooms and herbs. "I just want to talk." I pleaded, not moving any closer as the expression on her face changed from horror to cautious curiosity.

She wiped her nose again with her sleeve and glanced around. "What do you want?" Her voice trembled; her eyes filled with defiance.

"I heard what you both said," I told her, keeping my hands up so she wouldn't think I was going for a knife. I couldn't see any weapons on her, but I also didn't want to chance getting knifed. Her eyes narrowed.

"I heard you talking about how he did it," I continued. "How he killed your Granny and you don't feel right about letting me take the blame." I took a hesitant step forward. "Please," I pleaded. "Tell me what really happened. I deserve to know."

After a moment's hesitation, Red's shoulders relaxed and, to my surprise, she sat back down on the ground, the leaves crunching beneath her as she pulled her knees up to her chest and wrapped her arms around her legs. *I never realized how small she is.* I thought, remembering the way Fletcher had shaken her.

"I was home when it happened." She said, her voice quiet and shaky. She picked up a leaf between her thumb and forefinger and twirled it. "I was upstairs in the loft, in bed." She hesitated, then picked up another leaf and twirled both at the same time, resting her chin on her knees.

"What happened?" I coaxed, taking a seat a few feet away.

She didn't look up. "They were fighting. They always fought." Her voice was weary. "He wanted out, talking about how he'd never made the deal and it wasn't right of Granny to keep him bound to a deal he had no part in making."

She tossed the leaves away and studied the ground where they fell. "Granny didn't care. She laughed at him. Mocked him. Taunted him with what she would do if he tried to leave." She went silent again, as if lost in memory.

"What exactly," I said, clearing my throat as I tried to find the right words. "That is, what was your Granny threatening him with, or rather..." *Damn.* I wanted to scream, I pulled the top of my hair, frustrated with my lack of understanding.

Red turned to look at me, a wry smile on her lips. "You want to know what deal Fletcher was bound to and what Granny was threatening to do to him if he tried to break it." Her lips curled in disgust as she allowed her knees to fall to the sides beneath her cloak and picked up another leaf.

"Granny had a special box she used." Red continued. My heart pounded in my ears at her words. "It was a fancy puzzle box with the carving of a wolf on the top of it. A couple of drops of Fletcher's blood under the moonlight in those carved grooves, and Granny could control him."

My ears were ringing and my vision was blurring. I bit my lip to keep from passing out. "How?" I managed, my voice croaking.

"She could make him like you," Red speared me with her eyes. "She could make him turn into a wolf. Order him to kill, to hunt, to steal - whatever her cruel little heart desired." Disgust and fear permeated Red's voice. "Granny told him if he tried to run, she'd turn him from afar and force him to jump into a roaring fire."

Red shivered and looked away. "I don't know if she had the power to do that. If I had to guess, Fletcher didn't know either."

Trying to absorb what she'd just said, I nodded as though I understood. "So, he murdered her to get free of whatever bound him to the box," I said, more to myself than to Red. I shook my head. "But, why was he bound to her in the first place?"

Red laughed, angry tears springing to her eyes. "His grandfather made a deal with the devil woman long before he was born."

I gaped at her. *Devil woman.* The words rang in my head. *Cruel little heart.* "You hated your grandmother," I whispered, confused by the idea. "I always thought," I shook my head, remembering the few times I'd seen them together. "That is–"

"You always thought we had a loving relationship of kindness and harmony." She speared me with her eyes again, her voice mocking me with every word. "Like most people, you fell for Granny's charm. You believed my mild smiles and my ability to keep from wincing every time she touched me for fear of retribution when we returned home." Her voice was getting louder.

"Granny was not who you or anyone else in that gods–forsaken village thinks she was." She paused, still staring at me. "She was cruel and hateful, and I have the memories and the scars to prove it." Before I answered, Red scooted toward me, pulling back her cloak and rolling up her long sleeves. She held out her arms for me to see.

Horror consumed me at the sight of the marks lining her arms - dozens of burns and cuts, bruises much deeper than Fletcher could have made. They all stopped just above her wrists. "I'm sorry." Was all I managed, unable to look away.

"You should see the rest of my body." She whispered in return, pulling her sleeves back down and returning her arms beneath her cloak.

Unsure of what else to do, I nodded. "That's why he said she deserved what happened," I whispered, Fletcher's words making sense to me.

"Yes."

We sat in silence for a moment, both staring at the ground between us.

"I understand why you hated her." Was all I thought to say. "I would, too." An odd sympathy swelled in my chest. "I'm sorry no one else ever saw her for who she really was. I'm sorry they never noticed your pain." I bit my lip to keep from crying. "I know what it's like to be seen as something you're not," I whispered.

Her eyes roamed my face. "You want me to help you clear your name." She said it as calmly as though she were announcing dinner.

I looked up at her. We locked eyes. "Wouldn't you want your name cleared of something you didn't do?" Neither of us blinked as she considered my question.

"You know this means your grandfather never committed any of those crimes, right?" She said, not answering my question. "It was all Granny. Well," she paused and bit her lip. "Granny and my grandfather."

Anger began to mount as I continued to stare. "What do you mean it was your grand-father? My mother always told me that my grandfather was innocent."

"My grandfather was bound by Granny's box," Red said, shrugging her shoulders. "They formed an alliance long before they had a child. Long before I came along." She curled her lip again and looked away. "They worked as assassins and thieves. Granny used to boast about it to me, tell me all the gruesome details of their escapades while I cowered in a corner, hoping she wouldn't kill me."

"From what I understand," Red continued as my mind recalled each letter I'd read the night before. "Once my grandparents made their fortune, they returned here. My grand-mother was part of a group of Travelers that lived around these parts. They came back here and helped found the village."

Red picked at a thread in her sleeve as she spoke. "Whenever someone got in the way, Granny got out her magic box, grandfather got rid of the problem - as they liked to say - and your grandfather was blamed for it." She huffed and shook her head. "It was the perfect con. No one ever even suspected them."

"I don't understand." I bit out, my fists clenching. "I thought you said Fletcher's grand-father made the deal with your Granny. I thought he was bound to the box, and that's why Fletcher is bound to the box now."

Red turned to stare at me again, a wordless reply written all over her face.

"You mean..." I paused, blinked a few times in disbelief, then cleared my throat. "You have the same grandfather."

Red nodded. "Why do you think my grand-father was murdered?" She said, shrugging her shoulders, her eyes searching mine. "Your grandfather didn't kill mine. Fletcher killed my grandfather - his grandfather. All at the will of Granny."

"She found out," I whispered. "She found out he had another woman; another family." Red nodded. "So, she had him killed." Red nodded again.

"Please." I pleaded, inching closer as a spark of hope lit inside me. "Please help me. You can tell the villagers all of this. Tell them it was Fletcher." I held out my hands as the speed of my words increased. "You can explain about the fight, the box, your grandfather - everything."

Red inched away from me, staring at the ground again. "I can't." She whispered. "I can't find the box. Without the box, all I have is my story. No one will believe me. They'll think it's the stress of losing my beloved grandmother. Fletcher will kill me." Her voice shook.

"You can show them your scars." I urged, unable to hold it in. "Show them what she did to you." *I could give her the box.* I thought, opening my mouth to tell her. *The box might be the key to proving your innocence, your grandfather's innocence - it could clear everyone's name.*

But no words came out. They stuck in my throat, and I swallowed them whole as my stomach clenched with anticipation.

"No," she said, shaking her head. "Showing them her cruelty will only prove that she was cruel, not that she had a magical box that controls whoever's blood you happen to have on hand. Besides," she continued. "Fletcher will kill me if I don't leave it alone."

Red pushed herself up and brushed off her hands, backing away a few more steps in the direction from which she'd come. "I can't." She said again, tears about to fall from her eyes as she met my imploring gaze. "I'm sorry."

Before I could move or register her rejection, she was running, her feet crashing over the brush as she disappeared between the trees.

65 years Earlier
Celeste, 18

Autumn

Tonight's job was messy. This is the fifth time we've gone after someone on the Sheriff's list. With each catch, his respect for us grows.

This reward was larger than the previous ones. He asked us to catch a well-known thief, one I know by name. I eagerly agreed at the sight of the reward. After all, I already knew what he'd look like.

The job began like any other. We met under the tree, beneath the moonlight. I poured a drop of Evan's blood into the lid of the box, and he transformed into his wolf. From there, I gave him the handkerchief I snatched from the thief when he visited the pub.

Evan trailed the man like only a dog can. He followed him to his camp in the woods outside the citadel. We thought it would be easy. The man lay asleep on the forest floor, his chest rising and falling. Evan approached with caution, ready to transform back if needed at my command. But the thief deceived us. He wasn't asleep; he was waiting.

As Evan drew closer, the man turned and stabbed him. The knife glanced off Evan's shoulder. For the next few minutes, I thought for sure Evan would die. His only option was the fight the thief and kill him.

We got our reward, but Evan is wounded and silent.

He will not speak to me. I'm running out of ideas on how to make him see that none of this is my fault. I will not push for another job for a few weeks. It will give him time to get over his feelings, to forget the pain, and heal from his injuries.

Tonight was a disaster. Evan found the thief, a low-down piece of filth pickpocket. While they were on their way back to the Sheriff, he lost the boy. He claims the boy got the best of him. As though some kid with nothing to his name could outrun or outsmart a grown man who's transformed into a creature who can see in the dark and follow your scent for miles.

The Sheriff mocked me for the failure to bring the boy in. He says he won't give us any more marks until we catch the boy. Evan refuses to go. He claims he'll stay in one place and not move, no matter how many times I force him to transform or order him to track the child.

I've never been so angry. I've considered releasing Evan, letting him off on his own. But I would have to kill him to release him. If I let him go, he'll tell others about me. I'll be in danger. My box and me.

Frederick might even catch rumors of the box and come find me. No, there are too many problems to solve if I let Evan go. I must also admit, as much as I might hate to, I still care for him despite my anger. I want this for him and me - for us!

9

B Y THE TIME I reached Drina's wagon, it was dusk. The sun was disappearing through the trees. Drina sat beside the fire, stirring a pot of food. Children ran past me, laughing as they did. *What would it have been like to grow up here?* I wondered.

I hadn't found the courage to ask Drina why my grandfather left the Travelers or why my parents had never returned to them after my grandfather's death. *Were they unwanted? Forbidden from returning?*

Drina looked up at me from where she sat, searching my face. "I did not expect a hunt for mushrooms to take so long." She said, squinting as a forced smile came to her mouth. "Did you get lost?" she asked, still searching my face.

Dropping the sack of mushrooms and herbs at her feet, I stared at it as I realized how empty it was.

"I ran into Red," I said, unable to meet Drina's eye. "She told me..." My voice trailed off as my head swam with all the information Red had given me. "She knows I didn't do it. She knows my grandfather didn't do any of the crimes he was accused of committing."

"Sit, child," Drina said, a gentle hand reaching out to squeeze mine. She bent forward, twisting her head to try to catch my eyes. "Sit and eat. Then you can tell me all you learned."

I met her gaze and choked on unshed tears at the look of compassion in her eyes. Nodding, I took a seat without another word. She made quick work of the mushrooms and herbs, storing them away in the wagon. Soon, I had a bowl of thick bean soup in my hands and fresh bread to dip in it in my lap.

Blinking back tears that wouldn't stop trying to fall, I ate in silence. By the time I'd finished, my head had stopped swimming with panic at all the information I'd learned. I told Drina everything, halting intermittently to push down the tears I couldn't seem to shake.

Drina never said a word. She listened, thoughtfully removing the soup once we were both finished eating and placing a kettle of water over the fire for tea. The sun had disappeared by the time I'd finished explaining what I'd learned, and a chill wind had picked up. Stars twinkled overhead as clouds drifted by. I wrapped my cloak tighter around my shoulders and leaned toward the fire, watching as the flames licked the pot of water.

"What do I do now?" I asked, reaching out to take my mug of tea. The warmth of the mug chased a shiver up my arms and down my spine. "How do I prove my innocence if the only person who can help me refuses to tell the truth?" I paused, stirring a spoonful of honey into the scalding liquid. "Why won't she try to tell them all the truth? There must be someone who would believe her."

"You and Red," Drina's voice was slow and thoughtful. "The two of you have more in common than I ever dared suppose." She frowned in the firelight. "I believe I already know the answer to this question, however," she hesitated, as if searching for the right words. "Do you believe Red's story?"

I stared at her in disbelief. "How could I not?" I asked, shaking my head. "She showed me the scars, the bruises still there from the day Granny died." Anger surged. "Why would she lie about something like that when her Granny is beloved and respected in Fell Village? What would she have to gain from someone like me?"

"My child," Drina said, leaning forward to see my face more clearly. "I am not saying she lied about the abuses of her grandmother," Drina's tone was gentle and firm. "I do not doubt for one minute that the real monster among us all has been Granny this whole time. The letters you found prove that. This is what I mean by you two sharing more in common than I ever supposed." Drina paused again.

"But?" I encouraged her.

Drina smiled and took a sip of her tea. "But that does not mean everything she told you is the truth. Just as you did not tell her about the location of the box." She took another sip.

I blinked a few times, realizing what she meant. "You mean, there might be much more to the story than she let on," I said, nodding. *How is she already drinking her tea?* I couldn't help but wonder in the middle of my musings. *If I try to drink this, my lips will melt.*

"You must assume, unfortunately, that she is not trustworthy." Drina shrugged and took a long sip, as if mocking me and my fragile lips. "Red has lived her entire life much as you have: fearing the wrath and the power of Granny and everyone who followed her. She has never known safety or kindness. She's spent her entire life mastering the art of lying.

"The two of you share in the consequences of the choices that came before you. You must not assume that she will act in the way that best benefits you. While Granny's death might be your curse, for Red it is the freedom she's never experienced."

I nodded, feeling my body sag under the reality of Drina's words. "You mean you understand why Red would rather let things be than potentially ruin the first chance she's had at a life free from abuse and fear." I sighed. "I understand." I took a tentative sip and regretted my choice, flinching as the hot water hit my lips and burned the tip of my tongue.

"There is nothing else for you to do tonight, my boy," Drina said, a smile in her words as I flinched away from the sizzling contents of my mug. "Rest. More answers may come to you as you sleep, or tomorrow when you wake."

I nodded in understanding again, words failing me. We spent the next half hour in silence, sipping our tea beside the fire. The children's voices slowly faded, owls called to one another from the trees, and the rustling of small animals sounded in the brush.

Soon, I was in my bed inside the wagon, warm beneath the covers, listening as Drina's breathing slowed and her soft snore began. Drifting into oblivion, I found myself at a loss as to what to do, but with more peace than I'd known in years.

Grandfather didn't do it. It was Granny. It was always Granny.

Raised voices broke through my dreams. Somewhere in the distance, people were shouting. I sat up in a panic, rubbing my eyes to clear my vision. Drina was gone. Crawling toward the doorway curtain, I peeked through a slit. Morning had not yet broken; all I could see were shadows and the hot coals of banked fires.

"How dare you stand against the safety of innocent people!" A man's voice drifted through the night air. A calm voice responded, but not loudly enough for me to hear.

"You're granted the right to live in these woods with the understanding that you won't harm anyone from the village. We have reason to believe you're harboring a murderer! If you weren't, you wouldn't object to our searching your wagons."

My blood ran hot as panic began to set in. *I need to leave. If they find me, they'll kill me and everyone in this camp.* I backed away from the doorway, considering my options. *If I turn, I'll be able to see better. I can navigate through the darkness and outrun them if they see me.* I thought, reaching for that part of me. *But if I remain human, I can carry more supplies, and I'll blend in with anyone who's out and about.*

Ignoring the part of me longing to turn, I threw my cloak around my shoulders, grabbed my bow and arrows and my knife, then snatched up a sack and shoved as many apples and stale bread as I found inside it. On the very top of the sack, I placed the box before tying the fabric in one giant knot. Gripping the sack in my left hand, I stepped toward the wagon entrance and peered out into the darkness once more.

Shadows had grown as banked fires had been fanned into flame. Off to the right, a group of men carrying torches stood before the entrance of a wagon, yelling for those inside to exit. The sounds of ripping fabric and clattering dishes tore through the night air. My heart raced with anger, and the wolf begged me to let him out.

Taking a deep breath, I slipped out of the doorway and around the back of the wagon. The men yelled to whoever they'd sent inside the wagon while jeering at the family standing silently beside their home. *Fight back.* I thought, clenching my hands into fists as I leaned into the shadow of the wagon. *Don't let them mock you. Don't stand there and allow them to ruin your home. Fight back!* But the family remained calm and quiet.

"Child!" Drina hissed in my ear, grabbing my right arm. I jumped, stifling a scream. "You must run." She tugged at me, pulling me toward the trees. "Only a few of them came here in search of you. Most of them have had too much to drink. You must leave now before they reach our wagon."

Wet brush coated my pants with dew as Drina pulled me into the shelter of the woods as quickly as her body would allow her to move.

"I can't leave you all here," I said, turning to watch the men as they moved to the next wagon. "Why is no one fighting back?" I asked through clenched teeth, my sack of food hanging in my left hand as my right hand pulled away from Drina and moved to my knife.

"What would you have us do?" Drina whispered, not moving. "Fight back and watch them burn us to the ground? Kill them so we can be executed in the morning by the rest of the village?"

My shoulders slumped as I shut my eyes, defeat overwhelming my mind.

"To be a Traveler is to walk the path of peace, no matter how deeply you are hated and feared by those around you." Drina's hand fell on my shoulder, gentle and comforting.

"But you have others like me among you," I said, my mind reeling. "They could defend you, keep you safe from the cruelty of the villagers." I was grasping at straws, searching for any reason why retaliation wouldn't end in the complete ruin of the Travelers.

"They would die. Just as you will if you do not run." Drina squeezed my shoulder. "Please, my son. Run, and do not look back tonight. Keep the box with you. I will do what I can to help, as will the rest of the Travelers."

I turned to look at her, to argue.

"Do not argue, child," she hushed me before I could even try. "For once in your life, trust that what I'm saying is true. You are as much one of us as your grandfather was. We may not be able to keep you safe right now, but we will never stop trying to help you."

I hugged her, realizing how frail her bones were as I swallowed my angry tears.

"Run," Drina said, pulling back and clasping my face between her hands. "And may the Stars and the Moon guide you to safety."

Without another moment to lose, I did as she asked and ran into the darkness of the woods. And I didn't look back.

55 years Earlier
Celeste, 28

Summer

I'd forgotten about this book. It's been nearly a year since I last wrote. Evan and I have spent the better part of a decade amassing our fortune. We've moved from citadel to village, to citadel, following the money no matter who the payment comes from.

Things are becoming more difficult. I fear the Sheriff of this town suspects we've been behind the recent disappearances and deaths. Stories about our escapades are beginning to travel throughout the countryside.

Tomorrow we move on to a larger citadel. There's a local merchant who is rumored to pay a desirable sum for each successful job completed. They call him The Processor.

However, we will go about our lives differently in this citadel. I cannot risk being found out again. We're running out of places to go where the money is worth it. Evan will need to work and live somewhere while I live somewhere else. I've told him of this plan and he's agreed.

Evan doesn't argue with me anymore. I've trained him well. I keep telling him it's only a matter of time, and we can give up this life on the road, this life of death, and go create our own piece of paradise.

Things didn't go as planned last night. The job was successful, but someone saw us. Someone knows we infiltrated the manor and assassinated the lord inside. Someone knows we eliminated the farmer's daughter. Someone witnessed me transform Evan into his wolf.

I followed him. I know his face. He's a large, burly, red head. I've seen him before, but I'm not sure where. He was watching from the woods when I found the paper. I pretended not to notice him and walked on my way as if going home. When I was sure he hadn't followed me, I turned and followed him instead.

The man went into the local inn. I don't know if he's a worker, a visitor, or if someone hired him. The Processor must hear of this immediately. I do not want to become the mark of his other assassins.

 **10**

I FOUND MY WAY once more across the bridge, up the rocks, and into the cave I'd used before. For two days, I hid out in the cave, alternating between my human form during the day and my wolf form at night. Voices rarely passed by below, but the anxiety of being found would not leave me.

By day three, my food store was growing low, and my water had been almost completely depleted. Stiff from not moving, I left my cave before the sun rose and made my way back across the bridge, skirting the Traveler's camp to the North - away from the village.

Surely they've already searched my cabin. The thought had run on repeat in my head. *They've probably burned it to the ground by now. Not that it would take much to do that.* I was nearing my old home. The sun had begun to peek through the thick trees.

But if they haven't burned it down, if they haven't destroyed what I left, then there are a few things I could use. I stopped within the tree line as the small cabin and clearing came into view. Listening for any sign of someone nearby, I waited, biding my time.

Nothing but the rustle of small animals in the brush and the occasional chirp of a bird met my ears. Satisfied, I left the shelter of the trees and hurried to the front door. *Or what's left of it.* I thought, stepping over the shattered pieces of wood. Inside, I found what I'd expected, but it hurt more than I could have imagined.

What few belongings I had left were chopped into pieces. The few clay dishes strewn over the floor crunched beneath my feet as I took another step inside. The dirty clothes I'd left behind had been ripped to shreds and then hung around the cabin. *Like a threat.* I realized. *If we find you, we'll do this to you as well.* I shuddered. *Such hatred. So much vengeance.* Tiredness sank in, and I leaned against the wall, still surveying the mess.

My bed had been chopped up like firewood, the thin mattress ripped open. *So much for the hope of a little comfort.* I searched for my extra knives and the stash of flour I kept. My knives were nowhere to be found. Oddly enough, the flour had been left undisturbed.

They were too busy making a mess. I thought. *Or they poisoned it.* The thought came to me. I sifted the flour between my fingers, wondering if I should throw it out myself.

I don't have the luxury of throwing it out. Unless I can get more food from the Travelers or steal it from the village, I'm not going to be able to trap the way I normally would. I'll starve. I argued with myself, dipping a hand into the meager supply to feel the powder. *It feels like flour.* I lifted a small amount to my lips and tasted. *Tastes the same as before.*

Nodding to myself, I covered it again and searched for a sack to carry the tin container more easily. I found one in the corner, covered in ash from the fireplace and bits of wood. Looking around the rafters of the cabin, my eyes fell on a net I'd long forgotten. *Fish.* I thought, scrunching my nose in disgust.

Doesn't matter if you like it. Jumping, I hoisted myself up into the rafters to untangle the net.

My heart plummeted as a noise from outside reached my ears. I paused, one hand grasping the net, the other grasping the rafters as I perched within them.

"Oy, Sherriff," a high-pitched man's voice drifted through the walls. "Why are we here again? You don't think he'd be stupid enough to come back, do you?" The hairs on my arms rose beneath my clothing, and my pulse raced as I fought the urge to jump down and transform.

Dim sunlight drifted through the doorway and window. *Keep calm. They might not even see you. It's dark up here.* I tried to soothe my fears, holding my breath as a shadow crossed the threshold of the door. *If they don't come inside, they certainly won't see you.*

The boards outside creaked as another form joined the first, darkening the doorway even more. *Good, the less light the better.* I willed my heart to stop racing. *Stay outside. Please, stay outside.* I begged the figures I couldn't see, hoping they hadn't noticed the oddly positioned sack within the mess on the floor.

"Go check the woods to the West," a deep voice commanded. "I want to search through the cabin a bit more. See if we missed any clues and if anyone's been here." The other man grunted in response and shuffled away, muttering under his breath.

A man stepped through the doorway, and I clenched the rafter, my nails digging painfully into the splintering wood. It was the Sheriff, remembering how he'd almost caught me when I ran away from the crowd. *How did he catch up so quickly?* I wondered, watching him as he took tentative steps inside, his eyes surveying the mess.

"I know you're in here." He said, his voice low. My stomach clenched. "I just want to talk." He scuffed at the mess on the floor, as if looking for a secret trapdoor. "If I wanted to bring you in, I wouldn't have sent my man away. I swear by the Sun and the Moon and the Stars above, I mean you no harm."

I held my breath, considering my options. *If I believe him and jump, he might turn on me and kill me. If I choose to stay up here and he sees me, it might not matter.* I argued. *Better to jump and fight on my own terms than be seen and fight from above.*

Without another moment to lose, I threw the net over him and jumped to the floor, landing in a crouched position between the Sheriff and the door. He let out a cry of surprise as the net fell over him, pulling and clawing at it as he whipped around to look at me.

"Surprise." I hissed, pulling out my knife as I stood. "One wrong move and I swear I'll end you no matter what the consequences might be," I said, keeping my voice quiet.

"I just want to talk," the Sheriff whispered, pulling the net off his head and tossing it to the side. He sneezed, and I realized how much dust had fallen with the net. "Why would you risk killing me when I know you'll claim to be innocent of killing Granny?" he asked, tilting his head to one side to study me. He stood frozen in place, his hands held out on either side in surrender.

"I have nothing to lose. They already think I'm a killer." I scoffed. "If you think I would bat an eye at killing someone who wants to kill me, then you're a fool."

"You're right. I would be a fool to think that." He said, nodding.

We stared at each other for a moment, him taking in whatever bedraggled appearance I had, me sizing up how hard it would be to defeat him if worst came to worst. The Sheriff was a tall man, his hair jet black, eyes a deep green that shone even in the growing sunlight. His face and hands were tan from the sun, speaking to long days of work outside. His clothes were worn, but well-made.

"What do you want?" I said, breaking the silence.

"Did you do it?" He asked, not blinking.

"No."

"Would you believe me if I told you I believe *you*?" He asked, cocking his head to the other side, his hands still out in surrender.

"Why should you believe me?" I asked, my knife still ready to throw in my right hand as my left hand perched on my other knife.

"Because," a smile spread across his face. "Only a fool would commit such a heinous murder that quite obviously points back to himself and then walk up to the scene of the crime like nothing had happened."

I lowered my knife slightly, still eyeing him with all the suspicion I couldn't ignore. "Then why did you try to catch me at the bridge? Why go along with their cries for my demise?"

He took a hesitant step toward me, hands still raised. I braced and raised my knife again, stopping him in his tracks.

"I was trying to catch you before any of them did. To keep you safe." He said. His smile had disappeared. "By the way," he chuckled and rubbed his jaw. "You have a nice swing."

"That's a nice story." I scoffed, ignoring his comment about the blow I'd dealt him. "No one in that village has ever cared even a squirrel's tail about my safety."

"I swear," he said, raising his hands a little higher. "I don't want to kill you. I don't even want to take you in. I want to find the truth - to find who murdered Granny. To find out why."

I chewed the inside of my lip, torn between trusting him and taking him at his word or sprinting for the trees without the flour.

"What if I told you I know who murdered Granny, I just can't prove it?"

The Sheriff's eyebrows jumped and his eyes lit up. "Tell me." He said, taking a step toward me. "Maybe I can prove it for you." He took another tentative step.

My gut clenched, and I took another step toward the door. "That's close enough," I growled, a small part of my inner wolf escaping.

The Sheriff took a step back, hands back in their original position, eyes wide with shock. "I'm sorry. I know you have no reason to trust me or take me at my word."

"What if I can get you proof?" I asked, something inside me keeping me from telling him who had done it. *Just tell him.* A part of me urged. *He can confront Red. He can talk to the Wood Cutter.* But my mouth wouldn't form the words. Instead, I clamped it shut and waited for him to answer.

"If you can get me proof that someone else committed this murder," he said, his voice betraying annoyance. "Then I can help get the Villagers to leave you alone," he said, nodding.

"But I'll need solid proof. Not hearsay." He insisted, narrowing his eyes.

I nodded, lowering my knife. "I understand. Can you give me three days?" I asked, eyeing the net at his feet and the flour behind him. "Three days to get you what you need to prove my innocence?"

The Sheriff nodded, lowering his hands and smiling cautiously. "I can do that," he said, nodding. "Seems to me there's an awful lot of land to the North of the Travelers' camp that needs investigating." He said. "It should take a good three days to cover it. Keep people away from here; away from the Village."

I nodded in agreement. "Deal." I moved to the side and gestured toward the door, beckoning him to leave.

As he came to the doorway, he paused, turning back to me. "You understand," he said, clearing his throat. "If, after three days, you can't produce any proof for me, I won't be able to keep the search parties occupied anymore." He met my eyes. "You'll have to flee or risk being caught. I do not foresee a day in the near future when the Villagers will stop trying to hunt you down."

"Understood," I said, sheathing my knife. My jaw flexed with anger, but I ignored the sting of his words. "I'll get you the proof."

The Sheriff searched my face once more, then nodded and turned to leave. I waited, listening as he called for his man and the two of them disappeared into the trees.

Three days. I thought. *How am I going to get the proof I need in three days?* I sighed, gathered the net and the flour, and fled the premises.

55 years Earlier
Celeste, 28

<u>Summer</u>

Book, we found him. At the command of The Processor, we did not rest until we killed him. He wouldn't talk, wouldn't even utter a scream as we tried to force information from his lungs. I had Evan finish him off. The problem has been resolved, and that's all I care about.

A note was pinned to the tree tonight. The paper looks like what you'd find at a butcher shop. The writer claims to have killed The Processor. I fear this new assailant may be telling the truth. We have not received word from him since yesterday.

Our lives are threatened. We must leave this place. I'd hoped for more time, more fortune before we left this citadel. But if The Processor is truly dead, then there is little hope of gaining more wealth, and a high probability that we will die next.

We leave tonight. The moon is waning, almost at its weakest. The night is supposed to be cloudy. We will seek our escape beneath the cover of darkness. We'll return to some land I remember close to The Travelers. Civilization has not spread quite so far beyond a few farmers and woodsmen. We can create our own way of living. I can be a queen even if I never have the castle I dreamed of as a child.

11

I SLEPT OFF AND on all that day, knowing the search parties would relocate to the North. By nightfall, I felt stronger, my mind still rushing with ideas of how to prove my innocence to the Sheriff.

I could ask Red to tell him what happened. I thought, daring to light a small fire inside the cave as I cleaned the fish I'd caught. My stomach growled even as my nose scrunched at the revolting smell. *She might help me. If she knew she'd be safe, protected, she might tell the Sheriff the truth.* Hope would stir each time I considered this possibility. *But it would still be her word against Fletcher's. He might deny it all.*

Setting aside my prepared fish, I took a freshly cut stick and began to whittle down the point for a skewer. *Maybe if I gave her the box, she could prove she's telling the truth. She could show the Sheriff how it works.* My stomach clenched every time I considered handing over the box.

It belongs to me now. My grandfather made it. I shouldn't be giving it back into the hands of the family who ruined mine for no apparent reason. Bitterness and caution won over in this argument. I skewered the fish and held it over the fire. *A good char might help hide some of the taste.*

I sighed, turning the fish slowly over the small flames sputtering from the wood. The added warmth felt nice, chasing away some of the damp cold that clung to the surface of the cave. *If Red won't help me - if she can't help me - then I'm on my own. Why does this seem new to me when I've been alone most of my life?* I wondered, flipping the fish over again as it began to char around the edges.

Drina's soft bed, warm fire, and kind eyes came to my mind as I grew acutely aware of how alone and stiff I was. *I was alone, but I was also left alone.* I told myself, swallowing back the urge to cry as I watched my smoking fish and dying fire. *It's one thing to be hated and left alone. It's another to be hated and hunted down.*

Unable to leave the fish any longer before it became completely inedible, I pulled it away from the flames, hesitating to take a bite. Smoke curled up into the air as I waited for it to cool. *What if I tried eating it as a wolf?* I considered. *Maybe my tastebuds change with fish, too.* My wolf side pushed, excited at the prospect of emerging. *Why not?* I decided, setting down the stick and surrendering to the desire.

The cold in my bones disappeared as my wolf emerged, warmth filling every part of me. My eyes focused in the dark of the cave, the embers of the dying fire glowing brighter. I sniffed the fish, curious if the smell would make me want to gag. But hunger took over, and I bit into the meat before I even registered the smell.

It tastes...fine. I decided, devouring the fish. It was large enough to fill my empty stomach. After licking the bones, I carefully gnawed at the head so as not to break off anything that could kill me.

Every piece of meat on the fish disappeared, my stomach settling within me. I sat before the entrance of the cave, staring out at the rising moon. *If I'm on my own, and the search parties are to the North, perhaps it's time I went on my own hunt.* I thought, my eyes darting to the tops of the trees as they swayed in the wind.

If Red can't help me, then I must help myself and search for Fletcher. I'll make him understand. I'll force him to confess. My heart raced inside my chest as I considered the plan.

Why not? After all, if they can hunt me for assumed reasons, why can't I hunt someone I know is guilty? A satisfying amount of righteous indignation rose inside me as I got to all fours and trotted out of the cave, leaving my belongings inside.

If I were a murderous woodcutter, I thought, where would I go at night? I climbed down the rocks, jumping from cleft to cleft until I reached the ground. Starting off at a run, I picked up speed as I ran through the woods. The light of the moon hit my fur, and I felt a stir of something I'd barely taken time to acknowledge before.

What is that? I wondered, drinking in the feeling. *Comfort? Assurance? Of what?* I picked up more speed, energy coursing through every fiber of my being. Every time a ray of moonshine hit my coat through the thick trees, a warmth spread over me.

Soon, I was on the outskirts of the village. I came to a halt, ears perked to listen for any patrols. *They're on the other side of Fell, traveling to the North side of it.* I realized, wishing I'd used my wolf form longer when I'd gone to Granny's.

But where would I go if I were a woodcutter? I asked again, sniffing the air for any scent available. *A woodcutter who's also a wolf.* I told myself, closing my eyes as I took a deeper breath and searched for any sign of wolf scent.

Subtle notes stood out to me. Two different scent tracks lay before me: one leading into the village and the other leading into the woods. *That one must be mine.* I realized, excited at the prospect of using wolf abilities I hadn't yet explored. *Because I never tried.* I told myself.

Taking a step forward, I kept to a slow trot as I followed the smell across the bridge into the village itself. Skirting around the village to the South, I continued on my trail. As I reached the far West side of the village, the scent grew stronger.

A large house loomed before me, wood piled around it, shingles in disrepair. A single light burned in the second-story window as a thin trail of smoke escaped from the chimney above the room. The rest of the windows were dark and empty. No curtains, no light, no warmth.

I approached the door with caution, the scent of the other wolf growing stronger with each step. *Should I change into my human form?* I wondered, hesitating as I reached the door. *I'll be naked. And cold. Without any weapons.* The decision didn't take long to make. I'd left in too much of a hurry to have a choice now.

I nudged the door with my nose, hopeful it would open. To my relief, it gave way without a creak or any resistance. Pushing my way inside, I paused to let my eyes adjust to the pitch black, missing the warmth of the moon on my coat.

Above me, the creak of the floorboards sounded as someone walked across them. Dust fell as the footsteps moved to the other side of the house. *Fletcher.* I thought, convinced I'd found the wolf I was looking for. *I just need to find the stairs.* I pushed in a little farther, searching the dark room for a staircase.

Other than a couple of broken chairs, the room before me lay empty and full of dust. *No stairs.* I turned toward the entrance to the next room to my left, walking slowly and gently across the floor in an effort to remain undetected. Behind me, a trail of paw prints followed me in the dust.

Peering through the doorway of the next room, I saw stairs at the far end. A soft light drifted down them, as if beckoning me forward. I reached the stairs. A door at the top stood ajar, light flooding through it. *Why live upstairs?* I wondered. *Most would have chosen to abandon the upstairs and secure the lower part of the house.*

I placed a tentative paw on the first step, waiting for it to creak beneath me. It silently held my weight. Each step was more awkward than the last as I made my way up the steep incline. Reaching the door, I paused, peering through the crack to the inside. The only things visible were a warm fire at the other end of the room, a high-back chair before it, and a thick rug beneath the chair.

Pushing the door open with my nose, I took a step inside, cringing as the door creaked.

"You're late." Fletcher's voice came from the direction of the high-back chair. "I told you sunset. It's well past that." He growled, tapping his foot as he spoke. I took another step inside, my heart pounding. "Well?" He said, irritation overflowing. "Did you bring it with you?"

A low growl sounded in my throat as I approached, unable to hold it back as the hair along my back bristled. *He was expecting Red.* I thought, suddenly remembering the pity I'd felt as she told me of the hold Fletcher held over her. *He was expecting something else that could help incriminate me.*

Fletcher's foot stilled, and a hand appeared on the armrest, knuckles white as they dug into the fabric. "Who is that?" He asked in a low voice, not turning to look. "What do you want?"

I took another step, crouching as I anticipated his next moves. *What do I do?* My mind raced as I realized how little thought I'd put into this plan. *I can't speak to him. I can't ask him questions or demand that he admit to the Sheriff that it was him.* I growled again, hoping it would make him stand.

Turning in his chair, his eyes met mine. A shot of silver shone in the depths of his black eyes, silver I'd not seen in the forest as he argued with Red. "You," he said, his mouth twisting into a snarl. "What do you want?" He asked.

I growled again, wishing I could change back without being naked and weaponless, refusing to become trapped by a skilled woodcutter in such a vulnerable state. *You know what I want.* I thought, staring him down as I inched closer. *I want you to pay for what you did instead of setting me up to die.*

He laughed, catching me off guard. "You think I'm going to take the fall when everyone believes you did it? Why would I do that?" He stared back at me, as if urging me to answer.

Can he hear me? I wondered, shock setting in.

He nodded, raising an eyebrow. "Never lived among wolves, have we?" He jeered, pushing himself to his feet as he turned his back to the fireplace. He stood with his hands clasped behind him. "Well? What's your next move, dog? You want to know what it feels like to sink your teeth into a little human flesh?" His eyes glinted, the silver growing deeper.

I want you to confess. I thought, considering my next move. *I won't take the fall for you. The Sheriff believes me. He knows I didn't do it. He just needs proof. I want you to admit what you did.* I took one more step and paused, ready to pounce if needed. *Red will tell them the truth; she'll tell them how Granny tortured you both. She'll save you from the noose. But she needs you to agree so they believe her.*

Fletcher tipped back his head and laughed, his voice bouncing off the ceiling. "Red? Tell the truth? When has Red ever told the truth?" He shook his head, wiping away a tear of amusement.

"If you leave now, I'll spare you the beating you deserve for sneaking into my home." He said, taking a step in my direction, fist clenched. "I have no quarrel with you, kid." He shook his head again, this time with pity.

"You're merely the means to an end. But I can make that end come sooner if you don't leave. Now." He said, bringing his hands to the front as his eyes shone even brighter. "You will not win against me. The moon and I have been friends far longer than you. Its warmth runs through my veins even when the sun shines brightest."

He took another step toward me, dipping his head from side to side. "I'll give you one last chance, dog. Leave while you can still walk."

A million thoughts raced through my head, morbid curiosity making a strong case for picking a fight. But before I could act on that curiosity, soft footsteps approached from the stairs. Panic rose in my throat as Red appeared in the doorway. She stared at me, dumbfounded.

Sparing another glance at Fletcher, I darted toward the door. Red shrieked and hustled out of the way at the last minute.

This isn't over. I thought, bounding down the stairs as I battled the humiliation I felt.

"Don't worry, kid. I know." Fletcher's voice drifted down the stairs behind me.

I darted out the door and into the woods, relishing the warmth of the moon as I ran across the bridge and toward my cave.

Autumn

Evan and I have been hard at work. We've convinced the farmers to join us as a community, to become the village they will be. It took some sweet-talking and a few threats, but they're finally doing what we want.

The child within me kicks and squirms. I calculate I'm about halfway along. Evan says he's excited, but his eyes betray him. He's worried. I know not if his worry is for me or the child. We don't speak much. We spend the day working on our home. Evan spends his days in the forest cutting trees, while I spend my days hauling stones from the river. By day's end, we both collapse in bed and sleep until morning.

The struggle, however, will be worth it. We're building a mill. The village will depend on us to process their food and cut their lumber.

We'll never want again.

A local farmer got angry today. He didn't like the way we were going about clearing the forest for space in the village. If his defiance continues, I'll use the power I possess to create the world I desire.

Regardless of Evan's distaste for these things, I'm

acting for our own good. Someday he'll understand.

Last night I had to use the box. Evan resents me. He hates himself, but there was no other way. The farmer simply would not be reasoned with. He had to die.

No one knows where the wolf came from. They've never seen a wolf attack like that before. The man's family is terrified. They speak of the sheer size of the beast.

When they told me what happened, I quaked, crying and holding his wife to comfort her. I promised the village would take care of her as long as she abides by our laws and continues to supply the food we all need to survive. She readily agreed.

Loyalty may not be freely given to me, but it can be bought.

I had to spread the rumor. The idea came to me as more questions were asked, and more whispers began. I told them what I know of The Travelers. How they can transform themselves into monsters. How they have no control. I whispered back to their eager ears that the enemy might not lie very far from us. They accepted my rumors with glee – relief almost.

When the village wants answers, I must be the one to provide them. Even if the answers are a lie.

 **12**

B Y THE TIME I reached my cave, I was exhausted. I'd slept most of the day, but the extended transformation into my wolf form and my encounter with Fletcher left me spent. I transformed back into my human form, pulling on my clothing and cloak as I shivered in the damp cave.

Red won't help me. Fletcher won't admit his guilt. I can't force him. I thought, admitting the truth with reluctance. *What am I supposed to do? Leave forever?* The idea felt tempting. *Why am I fighting so hard to stay here when I was so despised even before Granny died? What's the point? Wouldn't it be easier to go somewhere no one knows who I am and start over?*

I curled up into a ball on the cave floor, cushioning my head with my arm as my shivering continued. *What does it matter if they think I'm guilty? Why am I fighting for acceptance from people who have reviled me for so long? If I went somewhere else, I could stop hiding in caves and living in the shadows. I might even gain friends.*

The idea excited me, producing a terrifying longing I'd never felt before. *People I can talk to, people who accept me for me.* I paused. *There's no guarantee. What if I go somewhere and they see me as a threat even without knowing my family history? What would I even tell someone who asked about me? A fake story, I suppose.*

The shivering stopped, my limbs finally warming within my cocoon. *It doesn't matter how far I run or how hard I try; I will always live in fear of being found out and despised or targeted again. I cannot be free so long as the lies built around who my grandfather was are still being touted as truth. If I leave, they win. It might be easier at first, but it's not a solution.*

I can't do this alone. I thought, a lump forming in my throat. *I'm so tired and cold. I can't fight them alone. I can't prove their guilt with-*

out someone helping me. Despair crept over me as the damp cave seemed to grow larger in the silence of the night. Unable to keep them at bay, tears of exasperation streamed down my face as I lay on the floor.

For the first time in a long time, I wished I could talk to my mother. *Someone who understands.* I thought, wiping my nose with the edge of my cloak. *I wish I could ask you questions - ask you what happened to my grandfather. Even if you didn't have the answer.*

I reached out into the void. *I have a sneaking suspicion you knew more than you ever told me - I was just too young to understand. I was too young to be trusted with the information. What would you have told me? Why did Grandfather make that box, and why did Granny hate him so much?*

The questions swirled in my head as my eyes closed and my breathing slowed. No answers found, only exhaustion. I drifted into oblivion.

I woke when the sun peeked through the entrance to the cave, landing on my face. Although I'd dreamt all night, I had no memory of what those dreams had been. My body ached from sleeping on the hard stone all night, but my mind felt lighter.

I need to speak with Drina. I thought, sitting up and rubbing my eyes. *It should be safe. The search parties have gone through their wagons, and they're all up North. I need to speak with her. I need help.* I pulled on my discarded boots and ate the very last of my simultaneously dry and molding bread, discarding the green bits.

Pulling on my weapons, I devoured the last apple I had as I walked across the bridge toward the Traveler's camp. I stood at the edge of the camp for a few moments, watching from behind a tree as the Travelers went about their morning routine, fixing breakfast, starting fires, and eating. Children ran and played the same as they had before I'd left.

This was a bad idea. I should leave before I ruin their lives forever.

"Where would you go, child?" Drina's voice right beside me made me yelp. A satisfied smile crossed her lips, but she didn't laugh. "Well, where would you go?"

I shook my head, leaning against the tree in relief, my emotions waffling between anger and wonder. *How did she do that?* "I don't know," I said, unable to think of where I would go.

Drina reached out her right hand to pat my cheek as her eyes searched mine. "Then we'll have no more talk of you leaving." She said, ending with a gentle slap to my cheek for emphasis. "Come, now. I know you've been surviving on crumbs and fish in an uncomfortable cave."

She started into the clearing, pausing to look at me when I didn't follow. "I don't have all day, and neither do you." She waved toward the North. "They'll come looking for you here again when they've exhausted their search up there. I have breakfast to give you and news to share." She turned to leave again, heading in the direction of her wagon. "Hurry it up."

Unable to resist the growling of my stomach or the curiosity of her insistence that she had news, I followed behind like a dutiful dog. *Maybe that's what I am.* I couldn't help but think. *Obedient in despising others. Obedient to the kindness of Drina. Just a dog either way.*

Drina whirled on me. I managed to stop short of plowing into her. She reached up and pulled my chin down to stare into my eyes.

"Never speak about yourself like that again." She said, her tone soft and stern as she raised her hand to give my cheek a gentle smack. "Not in my presence, not in the presence of any Traveler, and certainly not in the presence of those who seek to destroy you." Her eyes bored into mine, and I blinked back tears.

"You are one of us. A rare one - a child of the moon. And we will do everything we can to save you from execution." She slapped me again, this time a little harder, before pulling my chin back to meet her gaze.

"If you want to live - if you want to prove your innocence - then it's time you accept your identity as a Traveler." My cheek stung, and my stomach clenched with nervous tears. "Regardless of what happens, if you wish to have a chance in this world, then you need to leave behind an identity others pushed on you. Do you understand?" She kept her hand on my chin until I nodded.

"But," I hesitated. Drina tilted her head to one side, waiting for me to speak. "That is," I looked at the ground, shifting uncomfortably as I tried to form my question. "Why didn't you take me in before? Why didn't you take in my mother?"

Drina's shoulders visibly sagged at my question, and her face softened. "Your mother refused. She was afraid that harm might come to us if she stayed. Just as your grandfather had feared." She said, her eyes growing distant. "And you, well, we thought you died with your mother. I'm sorry, child."

I swallowed, pushing away the memory of my mother's death before it could overwhelm my senses. Nodding, I started toward the wagon again, Drina following behind.

As we reached the fire, the scent of warm porridge and wild berries met my nostrils. I sat beside the fire, my muscles relaxing as the warmth found me. Soon, a bowl of porridge was in my hands, topped with butter and hon-ey. I savored every bite, hoping I could one day enjoy breakfast with Drina forever.

Winter

Our mill is almost complete. Only the loft remains unfinished. The wheel turns within the river, and the farmers have begun to bring their grain for processing. They raise their eyebrows at the price, but I gently remind them how far they'd have to travel if we didn't exist. I tell them how important it is to support our community - how dangerous and time-consuming it was to create this mill. I push for gratefulness until they give me what I seek. They stammer and stutter and hand over their goods.

The village is growing rapidly. A baker has taken up shop down the street, buying his flour directly from our mill. A butcher is building across town, eager to purchase and distribute the meat grown by the farmers around us.
My plan is working.

Fear has grown surrounding the wolf attacks. I've had to utilize Evan several times to stamp out mutterings and complaints. He may resent me, but as I near the time of birth, I remind him it's for our safety.

If we are not in control, then someone else will be. We cannot trust that they will do a good job.

I continue to spread the rumors about The Travelers. Frederick came into town searching for me. The fury on his face sparked anxiety within me when I saw him. But I didn't back down. He asked me where the box was. I told him to leave before I used it. He threatened to expose me to the rest of Fell Village. That's when I knew I had the upper hand.

I told him the village would believe me and me alone. After all, where did he think the village came from? He should've picked me all those years ago. Instead, I picked someone more worthy. I'd been willing to let him alone, but not anymore. He'll pay for what he did to me, for the humiliation and rejection he inflicted upon me. He left, threats still muttered as he slammed the mill door behind him.

Tonight, another shall die. I care not who. Maybe that brat the milliner is raising. She just moved to town. He can't be more than a couple of years old. But the boy mocks me endlessly for absolutely no reason.

Whether he does or another dies, by dawn, I'll give the village a name to blame for the deaths among them: Frederick.

13

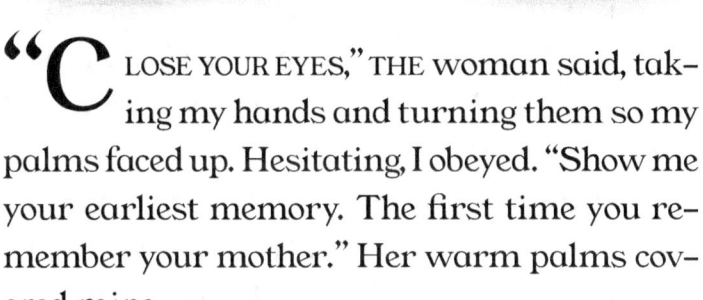

"**C**LOSE YOUR EYES," THE woman said, taking my hands and turning them so my palms faced up. Hesitating, I obeyed. "Show me your earliest memory. The first time you remember your mother." Her warm palms covered mine.

Drina had brought me to her wagon after breakfast. "This is Ruya," she said, holding back the doorway curtain for me to see the woman seated inside. I peered into the colorful interior, draped in woven fabrics of deep red, rich blue, and ardent green.

"Welcome," Ruya said, her gray eyes flashing as she met my gaze. Hair as white as the clouds drifted down her back and over her shoulders, carefully arranged with braids, flowers, and feathers. A thin bit of silver had been woven into one braid on the right side of her head.

"Come in, child. Come in and know your future." I'd obeyed, knowing I had no other option.

"I thought you were going to tell me my future," I said, as Ruya's palms hovered over mine. "Why do I need to think about my past?"

"You will never know your future until you confront your past, child," Ruya said, her hands unwavering. "Now, show me your earliest memory."

I sighed, digging into a part of my brain I'd learned to ignore. My mind flashed back to the first summer I remembered. I was running through the woods, laughing as my mother ran behind me. The panic in her voice didn't make sense to me. It was a game, just a bit of fun to make her chase me through the woods as I ran in whatever direction I chose.

I'd stopped suddenly, rounding a tree and running into someone's leg. Dazed, I frowned up at the man in confusion as I rubbed my nose. He stared back at me, his coal black eyes never leaving my face as one hand grasped an axe. Greasy black hair fell to his shoulders, unkempt. His face was tan, his shirt-sleeves rolled up to reveal his muscled arms.

I gasped and withdrew my hands, breaking the clarity of what I'd seen as I opened my eyes to look from Ruya to Drina and back again. "Is that?" I couldn't form the words.

"There's only one way to find out, child," Ruya said, her hands still extended. "Come back and show me."

My palms met hers, my heart racing as I closed my eyes. I was back on my bottom, seated on the forest floor, staring up at the man.

"Wolf!" My mother cried, reaching me within seconds. She kneeled beside me, wrapping her arms around me as if to hide me from sight. "Baby, you can't run away like that." She scolded, not even looking at me.

My ears buzzed as though someone was speaking, but I couldn't comprehend the words. My mother's voice rose beside me, but her words remained silent. The hatred spewing from the man's eyes was all I saw; all I understood. No words existed.

"I can't hear them," I whispered, clenching my eyes shut as though it would help me hear whatever my mother and the woodcutter were saying.

"Stop trying to hear them and focus on what you see," Ruya said, pushing gently on my palms. "What do his eyes tell you? What does your mother's body language tell you?"

She's crouched, I thought, letting go of their voices and focusing in on the way my mother kneeled beside me. *One arm in front of me, one behind. Her hair partially obstructs my view.*

I'd stopped rubbing my nose and was staring at the woodcutter through the strands of my mother's hair. His gaze drifted between my mother and me. My eyes drifted to the axe in his hand. His knuckles were white.

"Get up, Wolf." My mother said, quietly, still not looking at me. The buzzing disappeared, and her voice startled me. "Get up and walk back in the direction from which we came." I nodded, turning onto my knees to push up with my hands into a standing position. I brushed off my hands.

"Are you coming, mama?" I asked, taking a hesitant step in the direction of the house be–

fore turning to look at her. "Are you coming with me?"

"Go on, baby," she said, her eyes still firmly on the wood cutter as she pushed herself up from the ground into a standing position. "I'll be home in a bit. Now run!" I ran. Right before the memory ended, I heard the woodcutter's voice drift through the trees.

"Cursed blood. Death will come for you all, one way or another, the same curse that holds me will end you and yours."

My hands dropped, and I opened my eyes. "What does it mean?" I whispered, meeting the deep gray of Ruya's eyes shining bright within the wagon. "Why did he hate us so much?" I asked, wishing again for answers.

"Hatred has a thousand and one answers for why it exists, child," Ruya said, rubbing her hands together as she considered my question. "None of those answers is reasonable." She closed her eyes and covered her hands with them. "You shouldn't be alive right now. You should have both died in that forest." Her hands lowered, and her head tilted to one side.

"Did your mother return home as promised? That was not her demise?"

I shook my head. "No, she didn't die. Not until I was twelve. She came home later that night. I remember waiting at the door, staring out at the woods. She came home," I faltered, blinking with sudden realization. "She came home covered in blood."

Ruya's eyes practically glowed as she began to sway back and forth. "That was the day Fletcher's father died, and your mother kept you alive." She swayed a little harder. "By all odds, she should have died. He was stronger than her in every way. He could have shifted into a wolf and destroyed her in a matter of minutes."

I blinked, unsure of what to say. "Then why?" I said, not even able to complete the sentence.

"Cursed blood," Ruya said, humming before repeating it. "Cursed blood. He was not the owner of his powers. He could not control his own transformation. Which means," she stopped swaying and looked directly at me. "Did your mother shift?" She asked.

I swallowed. "I don't know," I said, quietly. "She never told me if she could. Never told me if she had." Odd shame filled me as I looked down at my hands. "Please," I said, frustration beginning to build. "What does this have to do with my future? How does revisiting this part of my past help me solve the problem?"

Ruya bent forward, a gentle hand coming to rest on mine. "If Fletcher's father could not control his shifting, if his blood is as cursed as the memory you showed me, then Fletcher cannot control his shifting either." She squeezed my hands and I looked up. "Which is why he wants the box."

"What about the letters?" I asked, frowning at the information. "Why did Granny keep those letters if not to blackmail him and his father and his grandfather?"

Ruya shook her head. "That I cannot tell you. Granny's motives are her own, and she took them to her grave." She shook her head again. "No, I don't see any desire from him to gain access to the letters. Perhaps he doesn't know they exist? Or perhaps," she tilted her head to the right, smiling faintly. "He might not care because all he wants is his freedom."

I contemplated her words. "You mean," I hesitated. "He doesn't care about exposure as long as he's no longer bound by the box?"

"Yes, and by whoever wields the box."

My heart raced as I realized she was talking about me. *I control his blood, his shifting.* The thought horrified me. *I could make him shift right now if I wanted to.* I glanced up at Drina, uneasiness flooding my mind.

"I must give it back to him," I said, shaking my head in exhaustion. "I can't give the box to the Sheriff. I can't give that box to anyone." Defeat was starting to sink in again. "The only thing I have from my grandfather, the only thing that might prove my innocence, and I can't keep it - can't even use it."

Drina leaned forward to grab my hand. "Take heart, child," she said, smiling. "There may be another way to free him without giving him the box."

"Why did your grandfather create this box, boy?" Ruya asked. I turned away from Drina to look at her, shrugging my shoulders. "I know you cannot tell me, but think. You have a mind of your own. Why would your grandfather create a box that could control the shifting of a child of the moon? Why would he carve out a box that could control his own powers if he wanted it to?"

I stared at her in disbelief. "You mean - surely he wanted to control his own powers." A cold sweat broke out over my forehead as I considered her implication.

"Have you ever lost control of your powers?" Ruya raised an eyebrow at me. "Isn't that what they've always claimed is the problem - that you and your family are unable to control the shift?"

I nodded.

"Do you need a box to control your powers?"

I shook my head, unable to take my eyes away from hers.

"Then why did he make that box?"

The truth was too horrifying to admit, but Ruya wouldn't let me ignore it. *She wants me to say it out loud.* "He wanted to control someone else," I whispered each word with a growing sense of disgust. "He made that box to control the shifting powers of someone else."

Drina, still holding my hand, squeezed.

"Only a monster would do that," I said, my lips and mouth dry. "Only a monster would take the power of another like that."

Ruya's smile turned sad as she studied me. "Sometimes the things we're told about the people we love are true." She whispered. "That doesn't mean your grandfather committed the crimes for which he was condemned and murdered.

"However," she leaned forward, compassion on her face. "It does appear he was guilty of something. Even if his plans never came to fruition. I'm sorry, child."

Unable to contain the tears anymore, I cried, silent sobs racking my body. I cried for myself, for my mother, and for whoever the box had been meant to control. I cried until I could cry no more. Drina's arms rocked me gently as she pulled the hair out of my face and paid no mind to the snot and spit covering her sleeves.

Ruya sat with us, unbothered by my blubbering. When the tears finally stopped, and my breathing calmed, and I sat up from Drina's embrace, Ruya leaned forward.

"We can fix this, child. It won't be easy, but we can fix it. Do you want to try?"

I nodded. "Yes."

20 years Earlier
Celeste, 62

Autumn

In all the 35 years I've lived within this village - a village I brought into being - I have never been so angry.

Evan has betrayed me. All these years, he betrayed me. I saw him with her, holding her to his heart before kissing her. Leaving her house early in the morning after telling me he'd be out running in the woods all night.

All those nights he spent in the woods, I thought it was because his wolf called to him. But it was because of her. It was because of the family he formed away from me. The milliner. That bitch who came to town with her son all those years ago, the boy Evan refused to kill.

It all makes sense now. The pieces have fallen into place.

I will exact my revenge. Before Evan dies, I will make sure he understands why he's dying and by whose hand.

14

I STOOD IN THE shadows once more, my breath slow and even, waiting for the guards to pass by Granny's house so I could go in. I'd considered entering through the back. But why mess with what had worked before?

Clouds drifted to hide the moon. As much as I felt the lack of its light, I thanked the clouds for their usefulness. Footsteps and voices soon approached. I sank deeper into the shadow of the trees and waited.

"When do you reckon the others will return?"

"Sheriff said they'd be away at least three days. It's only been two."

"What if he decides to attack us all while everyone is away? Clean the village out?"

They mean me. I thought, clenching my jaw in disbelief.

"I'd like to see him try!"

The voices drifted away as the footsteps disappeared. *I counted four. All together. The cowards.* I shook my head and pushed away from the shadows toward Granny's door. Testing the nob, I found it unlocked just as before. *Here's hoping Red hasn't returned.* I thought as I darted inside and closed it behind me.

My eyes adjusted to the dark space. *She's not here. She would've cleaned up. Everything is the same.* My eyes drifted over the rotten food, the dried blood, and the messy bed. I frowned. *That is, it's almost the same.* Something was missing, but I couldn't figure out what.

My eyes fell on the fireplace. *Do as Drina and Ruya told you to do first. Check the hiding spot again. Look for more.* Pushing myself away from the door, I walked on silent feet toward the fireplace, refusing to acknowledge the blood beneath my feet.

The brick had been removed completely and not returned. *Did Red find it?* I wondered. *Did she know where it was all along, but she couldn't get to it before I did?* I peered into the dark hole before sticking my hand in to feel around. *Empty.*

Removing my hand, I pushed against every brick, rounding the corner of the fireplace to check the other side. It was slow work, but necessary. *Nothing.* I went back to the table and poked around, gagging at the sight and smell of the food. *Nothing.*

Turning, I glanced around the room again, my eyes following the dim moonlight. *What is wrong with this picture?* I kept squinting, turning my head sideways to see things from a different angle. *The wood.* I realized. *The wood has been rearranged next to the fireplace.*

I walked back and started pulling it away from the bricks. *It was stacked before. Now it's leaning against the fireplace.* I laid it all to the side. A single floorboard was loose. My heart raced as I tested the wood, listening to it creak beneath my weight.

Taking out my knife, I pried it up. The board came easily. I sucked in a gasp as the hole revealed its contents. A leatherbound book lay before me, bulging against its ties. Beside it lay what I assumed was a tail. *A wolf's tail.* I blinked in horror. Underneath both lay thick, red fabric. *Is that Red's cloak? Why would she leave it here?*

My hands shook as I reached in to remove the contents. I was itching to read the book, to open it up and lose myself in whatever contents were there. But I knew that would be foolish. *I need to get back to camp.* I thought, opening the sack I'd brought and dumping the items inside.

Replacing the board, I also replaced the wood, trying to prop it up the way I'd found it. *I must leave before Red or Fletcher finds me.* My brain whirled with the possibilities of who had hidden the book. *It couldn't be Fletcher. It has to have been Red. Otherwise, why wouldn't he have taken the box the night I saw them both here?*

I headed back to the front door, cracking it open to peer out. Behind me, the back doorknob turned. Without hesitation, I exited the house and closed the door behind me, racing past the neighboring cottage toward the tree cover as quickly as possible.

The door opened behind me as I reached the trees. I expected someone to call out, but no one did. Instead, I heard footsteps following behind me. I picked up speed, running through the trees toward the camp. The footsteps increased in speed.

That's not Red. I thought, debating whether to transform. *That means it's Fletcher.* I picked up speed once more, pushing my body as hard as I could. *He was looking for something too. He wanted her to bring him something.* I ran harder, ignoring the growing stitch in my side.

"Stop!" Fletcher cried out behind me. "I just want to talk." His voice was breathless, but not as breathless as I knew mine would be if I tried to respond. Resisting the urge to look behind me to see how far ahead I'd gotten, I dipped through the trees toward the water. Fletcher cursed and pounded after me.

I need a plan. This wasn't part of it. But maybe I can get him to confess this time. I can threaten to transform if he tries to hurt me. I tried to ignore the doubt that I could actually attack him unless he was attacking me.

Even then, can I bring myself to kill him? They'd kill me for sure. They'd never believe he was being controlled by Granny to transform himself into a wolf. My freedom hinges on his confession, on the truth coming out.

On instinct, I whirled around and stopped running. "What do you want, Fletcher?" I hissed, more from a lack of breath than fear that anyone could hear me.

The man stumbled to a halt a few feet away from me. The clouds rolled away from the moon, as if on cue. Moonlight drifted through the bare trees, and my skin prickled with anticipation.

"I just want what's mine." He huffed, his eyes glowing in the dappled moonlight. "Red swore she couldn't find it, claimed Granny must have buried it or burned it. But I knew it had to be in that house."

"How am I supposed to believe it's yours?" I asked, my grip tightening on the sack. *I can't hand over this book. It might have valuable information that can prove my innocence.*

Fletcher shook his head and clenched his fists. "What kind of crazy person would want another man's tail?" He asked, taking a tentative step toward me. "Give me what belongs to me, and I'll leave you alone. I have no quarrel with you."

"Another man's...tail?" I stuttered, the realization dawning on me. I held up the sack and pulled out the wolf tail. "This is yours?" I asked, unable to contain my incredulity. "Why? How?"

"Give me my tail and I'll explain," Fletcher growled, taking another step toward me. The distance between us had shortened to arm's length. I held out his tail and he took it, surprise softening the scowl on his face.

"I don't understand," I said, letting my arm fall to my side. "Why did Granny have your tail?"

Fletcher looked down at the fluffy piece in his hands. "It was part of the curse." He whispered, his hands trembling. "My grandfather sold his soul to that woman. She bought my father's life and my obedience. She took my ability, my pride, and my tail." He looked up at me with fire in his eyes. "She deserved to die. I know it, you know it - why are you trying to prove your innocence to a village of people who care nothing about you?"

I stared at him, wishing I could call out for the sheriff. *Surely that was a confession.* "Why did she need your tail?" I asked, rubbing my forehead and eyes. Exhaustion was setting in as my adrenaline wore off.

"She had to get my blood somehow." He said, jaw clenched. "What better way to exert power and humiliate the dog than to chop off his tail while he was sleeping?" He tucked the fluffy tail into his pocket and squared his shoulders. "I wasn't exactly going along with the promise my grandfather made - the curse he inflicted on the rest of us. He had no right."

I continued to stare at him, wondering how to ask my questions without revealing I possessed the box. *Or his blood.* The thought churned my stomach. "Wait," I said, frowning. "Why did Red lie about the tail? Why not give it back to you?"

Fletcher smirked. "Fooled you, too, has she? She's as slick as her Granny." He laughed. "You think she cares about you? Let me guess, did she cry and tell you all about how cruel Granny was, even while she refused to tell the village you had nothing to do with Granny's death?"

He laughed louder as I flushed with anger. "Red always has a plan. Best you learn that now. Her plan will always look out for number one. She needed something to hold over me. She couldn't find the–" he stopped, cocking his head to one side. "Red needed something to keep me in line, to keep me from telling the village what a monster her Granny was."

I shook my head, the exhaustion growing. "I don't understand. Why would Red want to blackmail you?"

Fletcher grinned. "For someone who's lived under a curse his whole life, you sure don't seem to know a lot about them."

"Curse?" I asked, my heartbeat quickening. "What curse?"

"What else would you call being ostracized and blamed for crimes you and your family didn't commit? A happy accident?" He laughed, looking at me with inquisitive eyes.

"You're a strange boy. So angry at the person who hurt you, but so ready to believe and accept the lies of her offspring." He shook his head and sighed, turning as if to leave.

"Wait," I exclaimed, reaching out and grabbing his arm. Fletcher stiffened and turned to look me in the eye. "Please," I pleaded, letting go of him but not moving away. "Please tell the sheriff the truth. I want to live in peace." I paused, waiting for him to answer. He blinked at me, his face unmoved by emotion.

"You can clear things up," I continued. "Tell him I'm innocent. You can explain what a monster she was, how she made you do things you didn't want to do until one day you snapped."

Fletcher's eyes widened and his smile spread from ear to ear. "You think I killed her?" He tilted his head back and laughed. "I can't even harness my powers, boy. I can't shift into my wolf form unless–" His words trailed off again.

"I can't shift." He continued. "I'm still stuck under her curse, and I was very much still stuck when she died. You saw that scene," He leaned down until our noses almost touched, and I could feel his breath on my face. "You think me, someone under the power of that evil woman, someone who couldn't even harness his own powers - you think I'm her murder-er?"

My mind whirled. "No. I suppose you couldn't have." I swallowed, defeat beginning to wash over me again. "But if you didn't, and I didn't, then who did?" I asked, exasperation in my voice.

Fletcher stood up straight and eyed me. "After the way the village treated you and your family, do you really think any others who can shift would tell their neighbors?"

He shook his head again. "You really are dense. You've spent too much time living in the woods alone." His tone carried unexpected pity.

"This village has more secrets than you and I will ever know. If Granny controlled me and kept your family under her control, is it so hard to imagine she would have other enemies in this village?"

He turned to leave, pausing a few steps away. "Go back to your friends, kid. If you want the sheriff and the rest of the village to stop hunting you, then you need to find out who else in this hope-forsaken village can shift."

20 years Earlier
Celeste, 62

Winter

I caught him, book. Not Evan's bastard child. No, he's too old and wily. His wolf blood senses me every time I get near him, and he flees. But the bastard's son, Fletcher. He's recently come of age, just turned for the very first time.

As my daughter, Primrose, counts the moons until she gives birth to my first grandchild, Evan laughs behind my back as he watches his grandson grow. The betrayal is too much to bear. There was no other way.

I waited for the boy, late at night, beneath the full moon. Perched up in a tree with a net, I waited for him to return to his hiding place and fall asleep. As soon as he fell asleep, I ensnared him with the net. He never even saw me coming.

I didn't need long. All I needed was his tail, his pride and glory with the blood inside it. He struggled and howled after the net fell, but no one came to his rescue.

His screams were music to my ears, retribution for his father and grandfather, punishment for the betrayal of my love and faithfulness.

Then I let him go. I sent him home to his mother, that bitch who stole my husband all those years ago.

I have not bound him yet. I will do so tonight, beneath the moon still full and bright. I'll do so in a way that exacts my vengeance upon his grandfather.

Evan is gone. My heart is torn between anger and despair. It didn't have to end this way. If only Evan hadn't betrayed me, if he'd not gone away with someone else all those years ago.

I bound Fletcher last night, just as I planned. This released Evan from my grasp. He felt it, felt the moment his powers returned to him. Fletcher struggled against me, wounded and in agony. I admit his agony drove my vengeance forward.

Evan ran from me the moment I released him. He fled to her. The betrayal cannot be fully stated. I had hoped, foolishly, that he would come to me. But he did not. Somehow, he knew why I released him. His first thought was not to comfort me, to beg for my forgiveness. No. His first thought was for himself and his selfish desires.

Fletcher met him in the doorway in his wolf form. He fought me, but not for long. He cannot resist the magic of the box. No one can. Evan tried to run; he tried to escape and not turn to his wolf. But Fletcher was too quick. Evan made it to the edge of the woods before Fletcher caught him.

Evan is no more.

I will allow Fletcher's grandmother to live in fear. It's what she deserves, after all. His father can live on, knowing his son might turn on him at any moment. I will never give up my control, never finish reaping my revenge.

Evan is gone, and my foolish old heart is a mess of missing him and hating him. May his final rest never come.

I've cast the blame on Frederick. He lives a secluded life in the forest. The village is forming a search party. They plan to hunt him down and execute him for the crimes I've laid at his feet.

Good riddance.

I will let Fletcher alone for a little while. I need him to be stronger and older to fight against others.

Evan has left me, but in a real sense, he left me long ago. I just never realized it.

I cannot bear to look at Primrose anymore. I despise the blood of her father that runs through her veins. I asked her if she knew, pushed her to the brink of despair. I have my methods. But she knew nothing. Now all I have left of Evan is a child I hate and her unborn spawn.

Perhaps they should pay for his betrayal as well.

15

THAT SAME NIGHT, I left a note in Granny's house for Red to meet me in the same place we'd met before. I hoped she wouldn't just crumple up the note and throw it in the fire.

Sneaking back into her house was painless and quick. I tacked it to the ladder that led into the loft, hoping she'd see it when she returned.

When I returned to the wagons, Drina and I spent hours reading aloud from Granny's book. Each page explained more of who she was, a woman we didn't know or understand. But I still didn't have the answers I needed.

The next morning, I found my way to the clearing and waited. *Better to wait all day than come late and miss her.* I sat beneath some trees, my back to the trunk, twirling blades of grass between my fingers.

Drina had offered to come with me. But I was afraid Red would run if she saw anyone other than me. Drina understood, but the look of worry on her face was too powerful to be erased by an understanding smile.

It's too far for her to walk, too, I thought, *I'd be cruel if I asked her to walk this far.* So I waited alone.

Near twilight, I heard rustling and turned to watch as Red came into view. She searched the trees, her facial expression hidden within the hood of her cloak. I waved as she turned in my direction and pushed myself up to a standing position.

Glancing around furtively, Red came toward me, stopping far enough away that I couldn't reach out and touch her.

"What do you want?" She said, pulling the hood down so I could see her face. Apprehension and anger were at war in her eyes.

"I need your help," I said.

Red took a step back, shaking her head in exasperation as she held up both hands. "I already told yo–" She began.

"You told me a lie." I cut her off, and she froze. "You told me that Fletcher murdered Granny. But he couldn't have." I took a step closer, pulling out the box but maintaining my distance. "You know what this is and how it works." I wasn't asking Red about her knowledge, I was telling her. But she nodded anyway, her eyes growing wide with fear.

"Fletcher remains bound by this box. He swears he didn't kill Granny, and I believe him for one simple reason: he couldn't have murdered her because he was still bound by this box. Granny would never have commanded him to kill her. So my question for you is this: why did you lie to me, and who actually killed Granny?"

I waited, still gripping the box between both hands. Red continued to stare at it for a moment, the horror on her face turning to a look of disgust. Slowly, she raised her eyes to meet mine.

"How did you get that box?" She whispered, her hands clenching and unclenching on repeat.

"I ask the questions," I said, pushing the box back into the sack slung around my shoulders. "Why did you lie to me about who killed Granny?"

Red's breathing intensified, as though the very thought brought her distress. "I didn't think you'd believe me if I told you the truth." She said at last. "I recognized the man who did it, but I didn't think you or anyone else would believe me."

I laughed. "Try me," I said. "I believe a lot of things lately."

"There was someone there the night Granny died," Red began, her hands clenching tight. "He came into the house, just as I said Fletcher did. He forced his way in. I saw him through the floorboards of the loft. Granny never stood a chance. All I could do was hide and hope he wouldn't try to kill me too."

With a clenched jaw, I took a step toward her. "Stop delaying your answer," I said. "Who killed Granny?"

Red swallowed and took a short step backwards in return. "The Sheriff."

I blinked at her in stunned silence. "The Sheriff?" I managed to ask. "You're telling me the Sheriff murdered Granny? Why?"

My mind whirled with questions, thinking back to the day I'd spoken to him - the day he'd told me to prove who murdered Granny before he returned. *Why let me go if he did it? That doesn't make any sense.*

Red shook her head and shrugged her shoulders. "How should I know? Maybe she had him under her control as well. So many in Fell were afraid of Granny. She visited someone at least once a day and never came home empty-handed."

Red shifted on her feet. "Think about it," she continued. "Granny managed to make the entire village hate you simply for who your grandfather was. Even though he was innocent." She looked down. "If anyone else in Fell Village can shift, they wouldn't exactly publicize it."

I nodded. "Yes, I've considered that," I said, opting out of telling her Fletcher had said the same thing. "Why is Fletcher still bound to the box?" I asked, changing tactics. "Granny is

191

dead. If he was bound to the box by Granny, shouldn't he be released when she dies? Why is he still bound to a box when the one who controlled him is dead and can't wield it anymore?"

Red shrugged her shoulders, still looking down at her feet as she nudged a clump of dirt with her toe. "How am I supposed to know?" She said. "Granny didn't share much about how the power worked." A smug smile crossed her lips. "After all, your grandfather made it."

We stood in silence, me staring at Red while she memorized her feet.

"You're certain the Sheriff killed her?" I asked.

"Positive."

"Then I need your help. Please, Red. Nothing will ever get better until the person who killed Granny is caught. I could run," I acknowledged, clearing my throat. "And I've definitely considered that option. It would be so much easier to disappear. But," I hesitated.

"But the village will never move on or forget," Red said, her foot stilling beneath her and her eyes meeting mine. I nodded. "Fine." She said, sighing. "What do you want me to do?"

10 years Earlier
Celeste, 72

Summer

Fletcher's father has died. The rotten dog told me he lost in a fight with Frederick's daughter. I laughed in his tear-stained face. As if either of them deserves any better. Bad blood, the whole lot of them.

No one in the village cares. Fletcher and his family have been left to live on the outskirts of town ever since his grandmother died. He and his father made a living as wood cutters, not a skill many need. I make sure he gets enough to eat so he's ready and strong enough to do my bidding.

Beyond that, I let him rot and suffer his way through life.

16

I WAITED IN THE loft of Red's house, my breath shallow. Drina sat beside me, her warmth the only thing keeping me from coming out of my skin. Red had let us in as soon as the sun went down, slipping us through the back door while patrol was heading in the opposite direction.

Now we waited for Red to bring back the Sheriff under the pretense of new information. *What if he doesn't come? What if he turns on her and kills her and blames me for that as well?* My thoughts whirled as we continued to wait in silence. *But did he actually do it, or is she lying again?* I couldn't help wondering.

Drina had agreed with me when I told her I wasn't convinced the Sheriff had killed Granny. She was pleased I'd stopped trust-ing Red, as though I'd come back to my sens-

195

es. *Why would the Sheriff kill Granny? Why would Red lie about him killing Granny? Then again, why had she lied about Fletcher in the first place?*

I sighed and leaned my head against the wall.

The latch to the back door clicked. I froze, Drina held her breath, and reached over to grip my hand.

"Come in, Sheriff," Red said, lighting a candle. I peered through the floorboards. A brief flash of red went by as they moved into the house.

"What is this all about, Red?" The Sheriff asked, his voice sounding weary. "I've been out for three days and nights, and I just got back. I'd like to rest."

He's irritated. I thought. *Not suspicious. I suppose I'd also be irritated at being out for three days and nights, knowing I'm looking for someone who isn't there.* The thought made me smile.

"I know you did it, Sheriff," Red said, catching me by surprise. The house went silent. "You murdered my Granny." Still, no reply came. "You're using Wolf as a scapegoat. You know he's innocent, but you'd rather see him dead. So, tell me why you wanted my Granny dead?"

I blinked in confusion in the dim light, turning toward Drina. I could just make out the frown on her face. *This wasn't the plan.* I wanted to scream. *What is she doing?*

"How do you know I wanted your Granny dead?" The Sheriff's voice was calm - too calm. All of the irritation and exhaustion seemed to have vanished as a dark threat took over his tone. "Who told you that? Was it her?" He took a couple of steps forward.

"I-" Red sputtered, not seeming to move. "I saw you." She insisted. "You didn't just want her dead; you killed her. You're a wolf," her voice quivered. "You came here late that night and killed her."

"You're mistaken," Sheriff said. "I was here that night, but I was not the killer."

My insides froze at his tone, so dangerous, so unlike the man I'd met in the cabin.

"Who told you I wanted to kill Granny?" He said, a floorboard creaking as he moved toward her. "Did she tell you that? Did she know who I am?"

"Who are you?" Red said, confusion clear in her voice. *She's not acting.* I realized, the surprise in her tone was genuine. "Granny didn't tell me anything. I could've sworn it was you I saw here that night. Who are you?" Her tone turned angry within the continued confusion.

"I am the ghost of your grandparents, the curse that does not forgive." The Sheriff said, another floorboard creaking. "I am the vengeance of my parents and their parents before them. I am the result of time that has run out. I am a threat made good."

A cold sweat broke out on my forehead. *The writer of the note that didn't match.* I realized. *The reason Granny and Evan left.*

"You!" Red gasped. Stumbling sounded below, and I assumed she was falling backward. "You're the one she spoke of; the threatening note she kept all those years. That was your family."

"Yes."

"Then how can you claim you didn't kill her? I saw you change that night; saw you transform into a wolf. You were here, then you were a wolf, then you fled. Why are you lying?"

Shadows moved through the cracks in the floorboards as the noise below implied that he'd rushed over and grabbed her.

"Lying?" He screamed. Red whimpered. "My family has hunted your grandparents for years, plotting our revenge for how they destroyed our farm and murdered my aunt in cold blood!" Something clicked in my brain as he spoke. *The job at the farm, the farmer's daughter - it was them.*

"If you think for one minute that I'd choose to kill your Granny in a way that makes her a martyr while some other victim of her cruelty is blamed for her death, then you're the most foolish of her descendants yet!" I saw a flash of red as he shoved her away from him.

"Granny was supposed to live, to be exposed for her crimes," Sheriff said, his voice controlled even as he continued to seethe. "I spent the last ten years gathering evidence to show the entire village - evidence that could've freed Fletcher and then hung your Granny from the highest tree for what she did to my aunt, to Wolf's family, to your grandfather, to Fletcher - even to *you*. Yes, I know the cruelty you endured. Half the village knows, but they were too afraid to stand up to her."

He cursed and knocked something off the table. "I was here that night because I caught the scent of blood. Of course, I'm a wolf; I can shift. I prowl around in my wolf form all the time to track people.

"I smelled more blood than I've ever smelled in my entire life, and I came to investigate. That vengeance was meant to be mine. Now it's gone. Taken from me by someone who thought they had a better claim."

Silence reigned. I glanced over at Drina. The Traveler sat with her eyes wide open, darting back and forth as though she were considering something extremely important.

"The worst part is, Fletcher is still bound, and no one believes it wasn't Wolf." Sheriff sighed. "The evidence I gathered only worked so long as Granny was alive. No one will believe me now. Besides," he paused. "I'm still Sheriff, and I'm still bound to my oath to protect this village. I longed for Granny's death, but I longed more for justice. No one should have the right to take a life like that. No matter how much they might deserve to die, this wasn't right."

The silence in the house grew thick as I considered my next move. "If you didn't do it," I said from where I sat, my voice cracking as I spoke. "Then who did?"

"Wolf?" Came the startled reply.

"Yes."

"Come down from there." He paused. "And bring your Traveler friend with you. It's time we all had an honest conversation." A chair squeaked below. "Red, go fetch Fletcher. Don't try to run away or get the watch involved." He warned. "Go fetch the Woodsman wolf and come back with him. We'll be waiting."

10 years Earlier
Celeste, 72

Autumn

Primrose has died. She took her life while I was out. I came back to the sobbing child she bore.

In front of the villagers, I mourn and weep. I should be spending my last years with a loving husband and a beautiful family. Instead, I'm stuck raising a child I did not bear and controlling her bastard cousin.

Primrose named her daughter Firefly. I have always hated the name. I've convinced the town that red is the color of nobility and courage.

I've renamed the child Red and dressed her in a cloak to match. Regardless of who she is or who her grandfather was, I will be honored and obeyed. She will represent me and the victimhood of my family.

Red is the cloak she wears.
Red is the blood upon my hands.
Red is the blood upon the heads of those I control.

My mind grows tired, and this book is nearly full. This book
bears witness to my story. Good, bad, or indifferent -
I care not. Regardless of what my enemies might say, I would attest that my story is a good one.

Every good story needs a villain. Maybe I'm the villain. Maybe I'm okay with that.

17

W HEN RED RETURNED FROM finding Fletcher, all five of us sat around the table, the Sheriff throwing a couple of logs on the fire to warm up the cabin. Fall was quickly coming to an end as the chill winds turned colder and drove down from the North.

"Right," the Sheriff said. "I think it's time we talked. Because someone in this room is lying about who killed Granny, and it's certainly not me." His eyes drifted over each of us before landing on me. "I also don't believe it's Wolf."

I nodded, grateful he still believed me.

"So, who wants to go first? Fletcher? Red?"

The two sat side by side, glancing at each other as the Sheriff asked the question. Fletcher opened his mouth to speak, but Red was quicker.

"I'm sorry I lied," she said, tears forming in her eyes. "I knew it wasn't Wolf, but I didn't want the village to turn on me." A tear slid down her right cheek. "I knew it wasn't Fletcher, but I was afraid Wolf wouldn't believe me if I told him I saw you at the scene of the crime." Another tear slipped down her left cheek, and her voice quivered. "I'm sorry I lied."

Fletcher shifted uncomfortably beside her, as though he wanted to say something but couldn't. An idea began to form inside my mind. *Impossible.* I thought, cocking my head to the right as I studied Red's tear-stained face. *That's absurd. It can't be.* Her tears continued as the Sheriff studied her response.

"Tell me what happened again. From your perspective." He said, no sign of emotion or sympathy for her tears.

Red nodded her head, a look of apprehension filling her eyes. "I was up in the loft. Granny was in a mood. I got home late that evening and she–" Her voice cut off as she looked down and hugged her arms. "Well, she wasn't happy with me."

The Sheriff nodded. "I understand. Continue."

Red frowned, as though annoyed by his lack of compassionate words. "Well, I went upstairs after she, um, disciplined me. She was making supper and didn't want me in the kitchen anymore. So, I went upstairs to tend to my arms.

"That's when I heard someone come in the back door. It was a man. At least, I thought it was a man." She sniffed. "But then a wolf snarled and Granny screamed. It was horrible." More tears slid down her face.

"What did you do after you Granny screamed?"

"I froze," Red said, wiping her nose with the back of her hand. "I was so scared. I was afraid whoever it was would kill me too if they knew I was up there."

"And then?" The Sheriff's voice remained calm, cool, and devoid of emotion.

Red frowned again, fixing him with a glare. "What do you mean, and then? You know what happened after that. After I heard the back door shut, I came downstairs to check on Granny, and you were here!"

She pounded a fist on the table. "You shifted into a wolf and darted out the front door - a door I didn't even realize was open! But you want me to believe you weren't the one to kill her?"

The Sheriff nodded, not in agreement so much as an acknowledgment of what he'd been told.

"Fletcher?" He urged, turning his gaze to the man beside Red. "What happened that night?"

"Red came and got me," he said, avoiding the Sheriff's gaze. "She told me someone had broken in and killed Granny. She asked me to come help her. So I did."

"Help her with what?"

"I–she needed a friend," Fletcher said, his face contorting as he spoke. "She wanted to know what she should do since she thought the sher–iff had assassinated her Granny."

The idea in my head continued to grow. "So you arrived here *after* the Sheriff ran off?" I asked, unable to help myself. Everyone looked at me, startled by my sudden participation in the questions.

"Just to clarify things," I continued. "You weren't here until the Sheriff had already been here. You're saying Granny died, then Sheriff came here first, then Red saw him, then you came here? That's what you're saying?"

Fletcher shifted uncomfortably as Red blinked at me in shock. "Of course."

"Liar," I said, so completely sure of myself for the first time in my life. "You're still lying. And I think I know why." I said, glancing between Red and Fletcher. I pulled out the box and set it on the table, far from both their reach. Red's face blanched with fear, Fletcher's with anger.

"What is that?" the Sheriff asked.

"This is a box my grandfather carved." I began, my hands holding either side of it. "Granny stole it. Then she used it to control the man she married. He could only shift if she allowed him to. That man had another family."

I nodded at Fletcher. "Fletcher is also his grandchild, not just Red. Granny used the box to control Fletcher. She used Fletcher to kill his grandfather." I said the words softly, recognizing the shame and pain associated with every word.

The Sheriff looked from me to the two across from me. "And now that Granny's dead, can Fletcher transform by himself?" He asked, staring at the box.

"No," I said, shaking my head. "That's the thing, he should be free. He should no longer be bound by this box. But he's still stuck in obedience to it, even though the person who bound him is gone. Isn't that interesting, Red?"

Red fiddled with her hands and looked up at me. "How should I know anything about it?" She tried to smile, but her lips refused to turn upwards. "I never used the box."

"Liar," I said again, so confident. "You're lying." I smoothed my hand over the lid, Red going still in my gaze, her face turning bright pink with anger. "You used the box to bind him. You knew where it was. You knew how it worked. You saw Granny use it time and again. Once she was dead, you wanted to make sure you had someone to help you. So you did the same thing she did."

The house was so quiet. All I could hear was the fire crackling and the slow breathing of everyone around the table.

"How did you do it, Red?" I asked, my hands gripping the box as I stared her down.

"I don't know what you're talking about." She hissed, unable to shift her gaze away from mine.

"You know exactly what I'm talking about. How did you kill Granny?" I clarified.

Silence again. No one moved, all eyes were fixed on Red as her eyes were fixed on mine. Her breath quickened and her body tensed.

"You can't prove anything. All you have are theories." She said, her voice quiet. "Her body was ripped apart by a wolf. There were wolf prints all over this house. Pools of blood every-where - you will never be able to prove that I murdered Granny." Her eyes defied me.

Despite who she was, I admired her tenacity. "Did you sneak up behind her? Or was it poi-son? Did you sprinkle something in the food? No one would've suspected. It was all spoiled by the blood."

"You claim that Fletcher arrived after I did," the Sheriff said slowly. "That you came downstairs after you heard everything happen and found me here. But when you came downstairs, you were covered in blood." He eyed her, tilting his head to the left. "If that was your first time coming downstairs, why were you already covered in blood?" He asked.

"That was my blood," Red said, jutting out her chin. "From the punishment Granny gave me for getting home early."

"No, child." The Sheriff said, shaking his head as he continued to observe her. "You were covered in blood. You said earlier she did something to your arms as punishment. But his blood was all over you. And when you alerted the village to Granny's death early that morning, you were clean. Which means you changed before you told the village."

"How did you do it, Red?" I pushed again, watching her breath continue to increase as her eyes grew larger.

"She deserved to die!" The words exploded out of her mouth, shocking us by their sheer volume. "You heard Fletcher in the woods," she glanced over at me, a wildness to her look. "Granny got what she deserved. She got what was coming to her."

"So you admit that you did it?" I asked, my heart leaping within my chest.

"Yes!" She cried, a sob coming from somewhere deep within Red's stomach. "I killed her! She was a horrible, cruel woman, and I was tired of how she treated me." Another sob came shuddering out as she continued her confession.

"I had to. I slipped a knife from the table up my sleeve and pretended like I was going upstairs. She turned her back to me, grinning with glee at the pain she'd inflicted on her own granddaughter. I stabbed her in the back, pushed her to the floor, and stabbed her in the chest."

Red stood up, screaming at us. "I wanted her to see who put an end to her. I wanted her to know it was me!"

Blinking in astonishment, I realized that Red had stopped hiding. *She's telling the truth. Finally.*

"You did it," I whispered, blinking in disbelief. "You admit that you did it."

Red nodded.

"Before you went to find Fletcher, you bound him to the box again, didn't you? In fact," I paused, the realization hitting me. "That's how you called him here, isn't it?"

She nodded again. Fletcher was staring at the table, his hands clenched together, pure hatred shining in his eyes.

"He came here and you commanded him to help you make it look like Granny was killed by a wolf - by me."

Red swallowed and nodded again. I envisioned how satisfied Fletcher must have felt as he ripped the place to pieces, causing Granny's wounds to look like a wolf took her out. My skin crawled imagining the entire scene.

"It was you in the forest." I gasped. "You snuck up behind me while Fletcher had his way with Granny. You knocked me unconscious."

Red and I stared at each other for another second before she lunged across the table, hands reaching to grab the box. I snatched the box out of her reach before she got it, stumbling my way around the table toward the fireplace. Red yelled, but Fletcher continued to sit.

He can't hurt her, but he doesn't have to obey her unless she holds the box. I reached the fire and held the box toward the flame.

"Stop!" Red cried, her hands outstretched.

"Sheriff," I said, my voice breathless. "This is the only thing I have left of my grandfather. But unless you need this box to prove my innocence, I can think of no better place for it than the fire."

The sheriff continued to sit at the table, unbothered by the chaos. "That box belongs to you. I believe you should do with it as you like. If you burn it, I can still prove your innocence. Drina will testify on your behalf," he said, nodding in the Traveler's direction. "Fletcher will be free and, I believe, he'll be able to testify on your behalf as well." He turned to look at Fletcher, who nodded without looking up.

"It would give me no greater pleasure," Fletcher said, his voice low and strained. "Than to be free - that is, to testify before the village as to the truth of what happened.

But," he cleared his throat. "Only if I have your promise that I will not face judgment for what I was forced to do." His voice cracked.

The sheriff nodded. "You have my word. Testify to the truth, and I will not hold you responsible for anything you've done under the binding spell of that box."

Without another word, I threw the box into the fire. Red cried out and lunged forward, as if to grab it from the flames. But the sheriff was too fast. He stood from his chair, kicking it backwards as he reached out and held her arm firm.

All eyes turned to the burning box. I watched as the carefully carved wolf burst into flames, the dry wood crackling as it caught fire. The vial of blood burst as the heat got to it.

I turned to look at Fletcher. His shoulders slumped, and he held onto the table, tears pouring down his face.

"Thank you." Was all he said as he lowered his head to rest on his arms.

EPILOGUE

I SUPPOSE THERE'S NOT much left to tell. The sheriff held a trial in the public square. Fletcher made good on his word and told it all. I read from Granny's book, and Drina explained the way of the moon and the stars.

To my surprise, the villagers listened and believed much more quickly than I expected. A couple came forward, emboldened by Fletcher, and told their tales of exploitation and abuse at the hands of Granny.

Red was found guilty by everyone of killing Granny and framing me. Due to the abuse she endured, however, the village and the sheriff were lenient. Rather than prison or hanging, they exiled her.

The sheriff told her to gather what she could carry from the mill and go. If she ever returns, she'll be imprisoned and hanged without question. He told her to find a new life, a better life, a life where Granny does not define who she is.

Fletcher has disappeared into the woods to rediscover what it means to be a wolf on his own terms. I do not expect to see him around again for the rest of the winter.

As for me, I was invited to take over Granny's mill as compensation for the harm done to my family over the years. After a night of consideration, I refused the offer.

Taking on the mill would improve my financial position, but I would never be free of the association it has with Granny. Someone unattached to the nightmare of her legacy needs to take over that mill.

Drina invited me to stay with her for as long as I want. I still have ownership of the cabin, and I'm no longer in danger of being executed by the villagers.

I'm choosing freedom. I'll stay with Drina, work to fix up the cabin, and create the life I've always wanted. No more running or hiding. Now I can truly be who I wish to be.

I wish my mother could see me now, wish she had lived to see the truth told.

But I also wish my grandfather had never gotten it into his head to make that box. I can only guess at what his hopes and intentions were.

At the end of the day, we all have things or people in our past we're ashamed of. Whether it's a grandfather who tries to harness the power of transformation magic, or a psychotic grandmother who uses that power to kill and abuse, we're all caught up in the midst of cleaning up their mess.

The End

Big Thanks

To my husband, Brian: Thank you for never letting me give up on my writing. Thank you for reading everything I write, and cheering me every step of the way. I love you most. This book wouldn't exist without you.

To my sister, Corrie: Your art brought this story to life. The pictures and chapter art are incredible. I hope you know how proud I am of you.

To my Ellen twin: Thank you for believing in me when I don't believe in myself. Thank you for sharing my love of mysteries, and for understanding what it's like to write.

To my Mommy, Aunt Trish, Aunt Kathy, and my mother-in-law: I love you all. Thank you for always encouraging me to keep going.

To my Beta readers: I couldn't do this without you. Your feedback helps in ways you probably don't realize. Thank you for partnering with me in such an amazing way.

And to everyone who keeps reading my work: I appreciate you more than you'll ever know. Thank you.

ABOUT ELLEN

A S A CHILD, ELLEN dreamed of writing books, acting in plays, and going on adventures. She read books, played in the dirt, and sewed herself costumes as she got older. Adulthood took over for a while and creativity took a backseat. One day she recognized the longing to write again and picked up an old story. 18 months later Child of Shadows was born.

Ellen currently lives a quiet life in North Carolina with her husband, Brian. In her spare time, she enjoys sewing, gardening, spending time with friends, and watching TV.

To watch her journey, access full color maps, character name lists, and learn more about her, check out her website:

www.authorellenceely.com

ALSO BY ELLEN

A curse long hidden.
A kingdom in danger.
A princess on the hunt.

Sarilda is the only daughter of King Otto and Queen Ada. On her 16th birthday, she discovers she is to be married to a neighboring prince as payment for a debt owed by her father.

Desperate to save herself from a fate she considers to be worse than death, and her kingdom and family from war, the princess sets out to find her long-lost brothers.

Join Sarilda in this reimagining of the classic Fairytale "The Seven Ravens". Fans of "the princess saves herself" will enjoy this tale of friendship, sacrifice, and courage.

Available on Amazon and Barnes and Noble.

But even in death a story is never truly at an end... An evil witch thirsting after unlimited power. A magical book that controls nightmares. An orphan with a knack for storytelling. A warrior determined to make amends for the actions of his father.

ELLEN ES CEELY

The Slums of Shantu run rampant with poverty and crime. The orphans survive, protected by the mysterious Shadows who tell them stories of a faraway land where nightmares come to life.

The dog's eyes burned red, its bared teeth glinting in the moonlight. A spiked chain connected to the building was wrapped around the dog's neck, digging into its obviously starved body. It growled dangerously and lunged at me. Screaming, I held my arms out in front of me, trying to hold onto the idea that it was a dream. I wondered if I would be torn to bits by the only living creature we'd seen on this island. As I pushed forward with closed eyes and clenched teeth the barking died out.

Eliora, an orphan of Shantu, soon discovers her quest is far more dangerous than she imagined. But she is also more powerful than she believed.

Available on Amazon and Barnes and Noble.